"I've never brought another woman to this spot, Savvy," Sky murmured, his lips tenderly brushing hers as they sank to the soft earth.

"It's been my secret place for as long as I can remember," he went on, as his fingers brushed her cheeks. "But I wanted you to see it. I wanted to be here when I told you that I loved you." He caught her face between his large, rough hands and kissed her again with a gentleness that bespoke his feeling for her. "I love you with all my heart, Savvy." Their eyes met and she could tell how much he loved her. She smiled radiantly, knowing the moment had come when she could tell him of her love. But when she parted her lips to speak he stopped her. "Don't say it unless you mean it, Savvy, please." Savvy stiffened a bit at the undisguised pain in his voice. Had he been terribly hurt by someone that he loved? she wondered, loving him all the more for his vulnerability.

Sky tightened his arms around her, and drew a deep breath. "Sweetheart, don't ever leave me," he said. "I need you for the rest of my days . . . and nights. . . ."

WHAT ARE *LOVESWEPT* ROMANCES?

They are stories of true romance and touching emotion. We
believe those two very important ingredients are constants
in our highly sensual and very believable stories in the
LOVESWEPT line. Our goal is to give you, the reader,
stories of consistently high quality that may sometimes make
you laugh, sometimes make you cry, but are always fresh
and creative and contain many delightful surprises within
their pages.

Most romance fans read an enormous number of books.
Those they truly love, they keep. Others may be traded with
friends and soon forgotten. We hope that each *LOVESWEPT*
romance will be a treasure—a "keeper." We will always try
to publish

LOVE STORIES YOU'LL NEVER FORGET
BY AUTHORS YOU'LL ALWAYS REMEMBER

The Editors

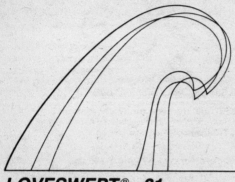

LOVESWEPT® • 81

Joan Bramsch
The Light Side

BANTAM BOOKS
TORONTO • NEW YORK • LONDON • SYDNEY • AUCKLAND

THE LIGHT SIDE

A Bantam Book / February 1985

LOVESWEPT® and the wave device are registered trademarks of Bantam Books, Inc. Registered in U.S. Patent and Trademark Office and elsewhere.

ISBN 0-553-21685-6

Published simultaneously in the United States and Canada

Bantam Books are published by Bantam Books, Inc. Its trademark, consisting of the words "Bantam Books" and the portrayal of a rooster, is Registered in U.S. Patent and Trademark Office and in other countries. Marca Registrada. Bantam Books, Inc., 666 Fifth Avenue, New York, New York 10103.

PRINTED IN THE UNITED STATES OF AMERICA

O   0 9 8 7 6 5 4 3 2 1

To my daughter Peggy, intelligent, imaginative, independent, idealistic, invincible. May all your dreams come true, Middle Button. I love you.

One

The sudden bone-jarring stop propelled her into the corner of the cubicle, and she knew. *She knew.* The elevator was stuck. She was stuck in the elevator. *Trapped!*

Wild-eyed, fighting the hysteria rising in her throat, Savena held her white-knuckled fist against her mouth. If she didn't start screaming, she theorized, then she wouldn't have to worry about trying to stop. Shuddering, utterly determined to master her overpowering fear, she drew a long breath. Fuming indignation became her weapon.

"*Well!* This shoots to hell seven months of intensive therapy . . . not to mention enough money to buy a new van," she muttered darkly. "*Dear* Dr. Winkle. Wait till I get my hands around your scrawny turkey neck. 'Ah, Ms. Alexander,' " she mimicked in his old raspy voice. Her fingers steepled in a pontifical gesture. " 'Your claustrophobia is cured. You will never be bothered by it again. I am certain.' "

To be honest, she had thought so, too, because she could ride in elevators these past three months with no ill effects. It was like a miracle! She had not been able to force herself into one of these small moving boxes since, when she was ten, her father had inadvertently locked her into a storage closet. She was playing hide and seek with him. He thought she was next door playing with her friends and he had gone on an errand. When he returned an hour later, he found her hysterical and completely terrified by her experience. From that day she was plagued by harsh nightmares and the fear of enclosed places. Finally, as an adult, she had taken matters into her own hands and sought treatment. She had seemed to be cured.

"Ha! Let's face it, Savena," she taunted. "You just haven't been in a situation to warrant a return of your old fears . . . *until now!*" In a near frenzy, she walked the boundaries of her metal cage, circling like a wary animal, seeking escape, knowing there was none. Repeatedly she banged and kicked against the walls in frustration. Gathering her energy, she yelled at the top of her lungs. "Mr. Goldblum! Mr. Goldblum, the elevator is stuck. *Mr. Goldblum! Do you hear me?*"

Faintly, she heard the guttural response of her

business associate and old friend. "Yah, Savena. I hear you. Do not be afraid, little dove. I will get help right away. Try to keep your mind occupied. I won't be long."

She exhaled in giddy relief. Mr. Goldblum knew she was here. Thank God! What had he said? Oh, yes. Keep your mind occupied. He knew about her fear and had encouraged her to seek therapy. He himself had gotten help when he had come to America after his release from a Nazi concentration camp. Everyone has some secret inner fear, he had told her. Well, she would take his advice. Keep occupied.

Glaring at her party equipment, she gave the tall helium tank parked in the center of the floor a decisive kick in its wheeled base. "You, O brassy barrel of hot air, are going to be my willing accomplice." With that brave command, she set to work filling balloons of varied bright colors. Each rubber vial expanded to eye-popping proportions, then hissed in complaint when she slipped a tight knot on its lippy end and fastened a length of glittery string to its neck. Like a mother hen, she clucked at her fat, round friends, watching distractedly as each floated to the ceiling of her cell.

"Hey, you guys! Stop your complaining. You're going to a birthday party . . . or had you forgotten?" She attached a sunshine yellow balloon to the tank and filled it with gas. Tying the string, she released it to float to the ceiling of the elevator. "Now," she said cheerily to the balloon, "you are for Katie, the birthday girl. You're bright, just like she is." She grimaced in self-contempt. "You're also the color of a coward . . . me!"

She pulled at a blue ball of light. "And you're for how sad I feel that I haven't overcome my childish fear. . . ." Then she grabbed at a green balloon. "You make me green with envy because I can't . . . and, oh, damn!" She touched a red balloon. "And I see red when I think about all the time and money and effort I've wasted."

Frantically she continued to fill balloon after balloon until the elevator was so crammed with the floating signals of her distress that they began to bounce off her head. "Gads! A three-foot-thick blanket of balloons," she exclaimed. "If help doesn't come soon, I'll be buried." Unaware that hysteria was taking control of her actions, she giggled wildly. "Hey, that's not a bad idea. If I get lost in a cloud of balloons, I won't know I'm trapped."

Her voice rose in dangerous octaves as she tried to hide from her entrapment. Her skin felt hot; her fingers shook. But she continued her task, methodically filling one wilted petal after another. Like a quavering echo, she began to sing in hushed high tones. "She was only a bird in a gilded cage . . ."

Her mind switched to automatic and began to replace her fear with fantasy. "*Superman!* That's who'll come to save me. He'll break through these walls like so much cardboard. He'll lift me into his arms and fly me to safety." Concentrating on her whimsical imagery, she pictured Clark Kent dashing into the nearest phone booth and changing into his Superman costume seconds before he came to her rescue. "Superman! Please hurry," she entreated in a whisper. "I'm . . . so . . . scared."

Suddenly through the blur of her fear and the cloud

of balloons above her head, she heard a scraping noise. Then a human voice filtered down to her ears. "What the—" a surprised baritone growled. At once her multicolored cocoon began to float out the ceiling. Someone—a man—had opened the trapdoor. Instantly Savena began to hop from one foot to the other, totally demented with relief. "Oh, save me, Superman. Please save me."

Most of the balloons had escaped when the inquiring face of a handsome male peeked down from above. A wave of sandy hair fell across his broad forehead and silver lights danced in his steel blue eyes as his wide mouth split into a generous, sunny grin. "Is this a private party or can I crash?"

Finding her tongue and trying hard to control her emotions again, she was nonchalant in her reply. "It's just me and my dozen or so alter egos. We were just passing the time until we were rescued." She gulped down an unexpected sob. "You *are* going to rescue us, aren't you?"

Without a word, her contact with the rest of the human race disappeared, only to be replaced by two Nike-clad feet. A pair of long, hair-shadowed, well-developed tanned legs topped by skimpy royal blue running shorts followed. With one leap, the remainder of this magnificent visitor materialized before her wide green eyes. She was not so addled that she couldn't recognize a rare specimen of male beauty when she saw it! The man's narrow waist and broad, defined chest was girded in a matching royal blue tank top. Tufts of golden hair drew Savena's gaze upward to his exposed chest and corded neck, then to his fine-hewn arms and large hands, propped carelessly on his lean hips.

Wow! her brain telegraphed in seven-foot neon letters. When her dazzled gaze locked with the man's laughing eyes, she gulped again, this time with a very different emotion. Actually she felt like an entire rainbow was exploding inside her body. But she held the feeling in and jousted verbally to cover her sudden inexplicable attraction. Well, not *totally* inexplicable.

"Nice of you to drop in." His grin widened at her play on words. "But didn't you forget your cape? In fact, you forgot your whole outfit."

His golden-lashed eyes narrowed while he digested her observation. Had this experience pushed her over the edge? he wondered. Then his sandy brows lifted in understanding. *Superman!* "I was in a pretty big hurry to get to you, honey." He chuckled gruffly, his measuring gaze sweeping her body. "I must admit you hardly look like the usual damsel in distress. You're a *real clown!*"

She frowned at his words and stood to her full five feet four inch height. "I'm Savvy," she retorted.

"I'll just bet you are!" His chuckle had a wicked knowing ring to it now.

"I mean, *that's my name.* I'm Savena and almost everyone calls me Savvy." She wiped her purple-striped sleeve across her face, only then remembering she was dressed for Katie's birthday party. Complete with whiteface and red fright wig, she *was* a clown! She forced herself to meet his dancing blue eyes. She was blushing furiously, but he couldn't see it beneath her painted face. For this, she was grateful. "Oh," she mumbled. "I get it now. I thought you were telling me

I was crazy . . . or something." She lowered her dark lashes and stood trembling before him.

At once the man stopped laughing. This kid was scared to death, he realized. She was trying to hold herself together with tough words and brave actions. Well, Brady, he told himself; *do something!* Before she falls apart right in front of your eyes. Without a thought to propriety or good sense, he stepped forward and gathered Savvy into his arms, hugging her to his hard chest and stroking her back with an easy, steadying hand. "It's okay now, Savvy. We'll be out of here in just a little while. Mr. Goldblum called the owners and they're sending someone to fix the elevator."

Terrified again, she grabbed the man around his waist and clung to him with superhuman strength. "You mean we can't leave right now?" She moaned, beginning to hiccup and whimper in renewed agony.

"Shhh, it's okay, I tell you. We can climb out the top if you feel that bad, but it's pretty scary. You see," he explained softly, "we're stuck between floors and there's no way I can pry open the doors to get out. Not until the repairman can move the elevator one way or the other. Do you want to try it?"

"No, no, no, no, no!" she babbled, shaking all over. "Just hold me. Hold me so tight I won't remember I'm still trapped." She felt his heightened embrace and hugged back with all the energy left in her. Like a drowning woman, she clung to his strong, hard frame. Like a life preserver, he encircled her body with a ring of security, helping her with his silent strength to fight her demons. "I don't know your real name," she suddenly gasped.

"Nobody knows Superman's real name, honey." He felt her stiffen in his arms, but he wasn't sure if she was bridling at his teasing or because he called her honey. Some women detested the trite endearment and he had been trying to rid himself of his innocent though out-of-date use of the word. "Don't say it unless you mean it," one of his dates had told him recently. Quickly he tried to make her relax again. "How about trying to guess my name, Savvy?" She nodded her head. "Okay, I'll give you a hint. My name is above us."

She rubbed her face against his chest, nuzzling his flesh, savoring his male essence, feeling his body hair trying to poke through the knit shirt to tickle her twitching red-painted nose. It seemed to Savvy she would never feel completely safe until she was out of here . . . or inside this beautiful man's tanned skin.

The man became aware of her movements. Her actions were totally unexpected, but certainly enjoyable. Pulling her closer into his arms, he widened his stance to take her full weight. It was fear, he supposed. But it felt damn good, remarked his awakening libido. Clown or not, there was a sensuous woman buried inside this voluminous outfit! "Hey," he chided softly. "You're not playing, Savvy. I said my name is above us. Aren't you even going to try?"

She was beginning to feel warm all over. Her solitary terror had fine-tuned all her emotions and suddenly she felt like making love. That was ridiculous! she scolded her errant desire. Forcing herself to think, she repeated his clue. "Your name is above us." Lifting her head, she looked into his smoldering blue eyes—had they been that deep and dark before?

she wondered—then glanced at the opening above and gasped. "Your name is *Shaft*?"

His hearty laughter rumbled from his chest and delighted her body. "I guess that wasn't a very good clue," he admitted, pulling her head back down to his beating heart. "You were supposed to guess 'Sky.' My name is Skylar, but everyone—and I do mean *everyone*—better call me Sky."

It was obvious she still wasn't calm when she giggled crazily. "*Sky!* And you just *dropped in* to save me. *Wonderful! This* is wonderful . . . and *you* are wonderful . . . and I'm beginning to *feel* wonderful . . . and—"

Each staccato phrase had risen in intensity and volume. There was nothing else Sky could do. He kissed her hard. He kissed her with everything he had in him. He had to, he told himself. The woman was about to go off the deep end. She began fighting him, and he held her firmly against his balanced solid length, closing off any avenue for her escape from his deepening kiss. Instantly she stopped resisting. With a wild, abandoned cry that vibrated into his mouth and right down to the tips of his curled-up toes, she surrendered and pushed against him, trying to make good her intention to seep inside his body to feel safe again.

Her uninhibited response to his kiss was like touching a match to a powder keg. He reacted like any red-blooded, healthy male would—he damn near exploded! His groan of surprised satisfaction triggered even more intensity in Savvy. When she felt his hard body respond to hers, she arched her pelvis forward while her fingers rubbed the contoured muscles of his arms. Dropping her hands, she dug her fingers into his tight buttocks, then ran her nails along the bottom edge of his silky shorts. She traced the side openings until she could explore the shape of his smooth, lean hips. And when she unhesitatingly thrust her tongue between his teeth and began an intense duel, he grabbed her at the small of her back and lifted her against his burgeoning manhood.

Erotically she rotated her body from side to side, exciting him beyond belief. Forcing her mouth to open wider, he plunged his insistent tongue inside and drank deeply of her soulful sweetness. Her knees gave way. Shuddering, she began to sink to the floor, whispering pathetically against his chest.

"I'm still scared," she cried disconsolately, burying her face in his shirt. Hot tears coursed down her heavily grease-painted face, melting into thick rivers of white that dripped from her chin. "It's not enough. I can't forget where I am. Help me, Sky. Please . . . *make me forget.*" Hysterical, she pulled at his strong arms. "Touch me. *Please,* Sky. *Touch me.* I need to know I'm not alone." Her words destroyed the last of his control and he slid into the corner of the elevator and pulled her onto his lap.

Fate stepped in and enhanced the moment—or threw a monkey wrench into it, depending on one's viewpoint. The overhead light went out. At once Savvy began to moan with fear, but Sky continued to hold her to him, murmuring soothingly. "It's okay, Savvy. That just means the repairman is here, work- ing on the elevator. You close your eyes and then you won't see the dark," he suggested, remembering a tired old line his mother had used on him when he was a child and sometimes afraid of the dark. "Have you closed your eyes?" He traced her lids and knew she was doing as he asked.

But then he felt her eyes snap open beneath his fingertips. "I can't do it, Sky. I'm terrified."

"I'll help you." He bent his head and kissed her, knowing instinctively that she would close her eyes at his touch. Passion took hold of her again as she surged against him, trying to blot out the debilitating terror gripping her soul. He cooperated as fully as any man could. The fire erupting between them left no time for Sky to examine his motives, sterling or otherwise. He ran his fingers lightly up and down her arms, then molded her against his chest while his hands massaged her rigid back. She pulled away frantically and drew his right hand to her breast, silently begging for his caress. She trembled against his palm when she felt the heat of his touch. Their kiss deepened and she moaned deliriously, tightening her hold around his neck when he rubbed his thumb across the nipple and then erotically molded it into full arousal. The pitch of her emotions brought renewed tears and she twisted around until she was straddling Sky's hips. The sudden shift of her weight almost brought tears of frustration to Sky's eyes!

"No, Savvy. This isn't going to work. It feels too damn good to me," he said hoarsely. He was gasping for breath, making low keening sounds each time he inhaled. His control was draining from him just as if someone had pulled the plug on his boiling emotions. Gritting his teeth, he lowered her to the floor and lay down alongside her writhing body. Knowing there had to be a way inside her billowing clown suit, he feverishly ran his fingers along the front and found a zipper. Her hands continued to move across his chest. When this action didn't satisfy her need for bodily contact, she yanked the shirt from his shorts, purring when she could smooth her fingers over his coarse chest hair and trace his flat, hard nipples.

Breathing raggedly, Sky bent over Savvy's warm body and slipped his hand inside her costume. He choked on his sucked-in breath and felt a white-hot coil of desire knot in his gut when he came into contact with bare skin. She was only wearing a lacy bra and skimpy panties beneath the clown suit. His sure touch drove Savvy into a frenzy. She pulled him hard against her and, at the same time, lifted her face and searched for his lips. For an instant Sky became so unhinged he thought he would self-destruct, even though he had been careful to keep his torso curved away from her undulating hips. Then he stopped thinking and began to move on instinct alone, deepening the kiss.

Please don't let the light come back on until this is finished, he pleaded silently. She says this is what she needs. Let me help her . . . before she comes back down to earth. It's going to be bad enough as it is. Don't let her be humiliated by an interruption.

Again Fate smiled. The pair remained secreted in the darkness. Savvy never stopped massaging his hard muscles or tracing designs on his hair-matted chest. Sky knew she was trying desperately to mask her panic with passion, but he sensed she was being only partially successful. Reality kept intruding; she still remained trapped in a black box. If only there was some way he could help her escape mentally . . .

"Savvy, I'm going to take you on a little trip in your mind. I want you to picture in your mind the secret place I'm going to tell you about. Come with me and I'll set you free. Do you understand what I'm saying, Savvy?" She nodded and he began speaking while gently stroking her warm, responsive skin.

"Picture a wide meadow thick with green grasses blowing in a gentle wind. You can feel the sun and the breeze on your skin. It cools you and warms you at the same time. Look around you. See the wild flowers? There are bluebells and black-eyed Susans . . . and over there is a big old oak tree just waiting to shade us from the noonday sun." As he spoke he could feel her tension melting away, and he continued to stroke her firm breasts with a sure, sensitizing touch. "Let's walk over to the tree, Savvy. Walk by my side and feel the long meadow grass tickle your bare legs. Watch out for that gopher hole!" He was rewarded by a tiny giggle for his efforts. "Now lie down with me. Lie in my arms and look around you. You can see across the flat land for miles until the earth touches the sky on the horizon. We're alone in this place. So wide, so big, so free. There are no fences here, only freedom. We can fly up into the sky and play among the fleecy clouds. Come fly with me, Savvy."

His words were a whisper on a summer breeze. Then his touch changed and her flesh responded. She began to moan softly. Sky's mouth captured her throaty sighs and muted the sound. No one could know this was happening. Never would anyone ever have the chance to guess what was taking place on the floor of an antiquated dark elevator. It would be their secret. Sky just hoped she wouldn't hate him later.

He bent to his heavenly task, worshiping her breasts, circling her hard peaks, wondering if he would ever have the opportunity to see if they were rosy and smoke-tinted. He let his imagination conjure a vision of her naked body stretched in feline grace upon a bed of milky silk sheets. His heart drummed, matching her wild rhythm. If only he could be sure they'd not be interrupted, he thought, almost out of his mind with his desire to possess her.

No thoughts entered Savvy's mind. Her body had taken over her fear and was controlling her actions completely. When she felt Sky's hand trail lower, she unhesitatingly moved her legs and welcomed his touch. She wasn't thinking. She never wanted to think again. She only wanted to feel. And it was just as well, because his touch was magic. Her responsive body shuddered and coiled beneath his heaving chest while he pressed against her warm breasts, holding her firmly, securely, safely. It felt so right to be held in his arms. His warm mouth continued to cover hers, catching within all sounds she made. Slowly, slowly she relaxed, her earlier hysteria replaced by a languorous contentment.

By the time the light came on again, Sky had refastened her clothing and was cradling her tenderly in his arms as they sat in the corner of the elevator. He kissed the tip of her red nose and smiled bemusedly down at her tear-streaked funnyface. His thoughts were bemused as well. He was certain he wouldn't ever set foot in another elevator without remembering this one!

Then he heard noises above him and knew he had to prepare himself to deal with Savvy's feelings when she realized how she had reacted to him. He only hoped she wouldn't be too hard on herself. For him, it had been ecstatic duty!

"Hey! You people all right down there?" a gravelly voice called down from the elevator shaft above them.

"Yeah, Mac. We're fine," Sky answered. He braced his back against the metal wall and effortlessly rose to his feet, bringing Savvy's limp body along with him. "Well, how about it, old man?" he added. "You gonna get this thing movin'?"

"I mighta knowed it was you, Brady. You're a regular white knight, ain't cha? Always there when trouble comes." The man laughed knowingly. "You can move anytime you press the down button, *Skylar*!" He laughed again, good-naturedly enjoying his opportunity to get Brady's goat without paying the penalty.

"Wait till the next time you want a favor, Henry." Sky leaned around Savvy and pushed the ivory circle marked "G." With a bone-rattling jerk, the elevator began its slow descent. He felt his companion's apprehensive shudder and bent to her ear. "It's going to be all right, Savvy. We're almost out of here."

Life was beginning to come back into Savvy's body. She still felt as if she were caught in some sort of time warp, but she lifted her heavy-lidded eyes to look— really look—at her rescuer. When she focused on his face so close to hers, she gasped in dismay. "Your face! And your neck! And your chest! You're covered with my makeup."

Sky glanced down with an exasperated frown. "Damn! That's all I need. I'll be razzed for weeks."

"Quick! Let me help." She yanked the Velcro-fastened ruffled collar from her costume and began frantically to rub the purple fabric over the white and red and black marks smeared across his skin. "Oh, I wish I had some cold cream," she lamented, scrubbing his mouth and neck. Although she was working rapidly, she was grateful it was taking a rather long time to reach the ground floor. Then she saw his shirt. "Your top! It's all messed up too."

"I can take care of that. Step back." With lightning speed Sky pulled the shirt off, turned it inside out, and jammed it back on. Tucking the tail into his shorts, he sighed in relief. "There. That should stop most of the hecklers."

When he looked again at Savvy, she was wringing her hands and moaning softly. Well, Brady, this is it, he told himself. She's starting to remember . . . and she probably feels like hell! He reached over and gently patted her shoulder. "Hey! Stop thinking. You were in shock and scared to death."

She continued to abuse her trembling hands. "Oh, my heavens! I'm so ashamed. *I could just die!*" When he tried to take her hand, she jumped back as if his touch burned her skin.

"If you get hysterical again, I'll have to use a different tactic this time . . . like dump you in ice water." He grinned impishly when he caught her nervous giggle. "Come on, now. Forget it. You came through with flying colors. And by the looks of that collar, so did I!" She laughed outright this time, much to Sky's relief. He just hoped her sense of humor would keep her glued together when the doors opened and she had to face the crowd of interested onlookers he felt certain would meet them. "Just forget that anything happened," he said. Then the doors slid apart.

"Savena, my little dove. Are you all right? I was so worried about you. I just hoped Sky would help you." With concern, Mr. Goldblum examined her distressed features. Unaware of the truth of his statement, he thought she was crumbling before him with fear, not humiliation. "There, there, my dear. You're safe now."

With easy command, Sky ordered a path to be opened to the exit and grabbed Savvy around her waist and led her outside. Mr. Goldblum was holding her hand and clucking paternally at her other side. Out on the shaded sidewalk she breathed deeply despite the summer heat and tried to control her inner turmoil. After a few minutes she turned to walk back into the building. "My tank and my box of balloons. I have to get them into my van. Katie's birthday party."

"I don't think you're in any condition to drive," countered Sky quietly. "You've had quite a scare."

"I can't disappoint Katie," she said with artificial calm. "I have a job to do." In moments, with Sky's help, she loaded her cargo and climbed in behind the wheel. Her body was still throbbing with unreasonable fear and unacceptable passion. She couldn't bring herself to meet Sky's direct, concerned gaze. "I . . . I want you to know, Mr. Brady, that I've never been so embarrassed in my life." Her stuttering words were barely audible to Sky. "I can't explain my . . . my actions, even to myself. Please forgive me. I know I forced you into a very uncomfortable situation."

His gruff chuckle made her head jerk up. "Now, *that's* a fact I can't deny, Savvy. Next time let's dispense with the costume and all that sticky makeup."

Tears were blinding her, but she threw the van into gear. "There won't be a next time, Mr. Brady. I'm not like that." Jamming her foot on the gas pedal, she shot away, but not before she heard Sky's answer crashing into her brain.

"Don't you think I know that, woman?"

How she arrived at the birthday party in one piece was a mystery Savvy didn't bother trying to unravel. She drove like a robot to the address. Before she got out, she wiggled through the front seats and hurriedly changed into her other costume, another purple one, this time in dots. Her mind was careening with hazardous thoughts. How in the world could she ever have let herself go like that? she silently condemned herself. She had made a complete fool of herself, and wished never to see Mr. Skylar Brady again. She could never face his knowing look. He must be enjoying himself about now, replaying their unplanned rendezvous. *Did I actually beg him to touch me?* How could she have done such a thing? Was it only fear? she asked honestly. Hadn't she thought he was a real hunk when he'd dropped through that hole in the ceiling? But she had been scared senseless, too, she argued.

In anguish, she reapplied her whiteface and tugged at her red fright wig, which had slipped askew. You idiot, she scolded. When you gave up control over your crazy claustrophobia, you surrendered everything else too. He probably thinks you're some kind of streetwalker with a new kinky twist—costumed sex! That last thought hurt more than she could admit. Shoving her abused brain into overdrive, she jumped out the back of her van and went on with the show. Above all else, she couldn't disappoint her little friend Katie. It was her birthday.

Meanwhile Sky recrossed the busy downtown street to the gym where his old friend Mr. Goldblum had found him earlier. After he went into the men's room to wash away the last traces of theatrical paint and change shirts, he began to run around the inside track that circled above the large room. Effortlessly he let his body take over. His stride lengthened and he began to think.

Now why the hell had he told her there would be a next time? He had just told her to forget it. He didn't even know who she was. He couldn't even guess what she looked like without all that goo on her face.

Ah, but you know what she *feels like*, reminded his pulsating loins. She feels satiny smooth. She feels soft and trembly. And she's filled with white-hot fire.

He gasped more at the thought than from the exertion of running. Had he ever felt a more willing partner beneath his touch? In the darkness, he had forgotten he was answering the plea of a terrified woman in a gaudy clown suit. Feverishly he forced his pace to quicken. He had never felt so unfulfilled. Run it off, Brady, he ordered. He had to forget about it. Forget that he wanted to experience her vibrations intimately. She wouldn't come within ten miles of him now. She had practically told him she never wanted to see him again. Yeah, but what could making love to her be like if she relented? he wondered. *Heaven!*

And he ran and ran in circles until he was ready to drop from exhaustion. His tireless mind, however, had not wavered one iota from its insistent train of thought. Was his light-headed feeling due to lack of oxygen, or was it because he continued to think about Savvy, the sexiest clown in town?

Two

Week followed sweltering week until the hot August sun slowed Tulsa's rapid everyday momentum to a snail's pace. Every living thing withdrew from the unrelenting heat wave. Rain had not fallen in a month, not even a light shower. There seemed no respite in sight, and Savvy melted beneath her clown makeup whenever she entertained at an afternoon birthday party or peddled her luminous floating baubles at an outdoor function.

Even when she jogged each morning at six o'clock with her close friend Teri Pegasus, she was drenched in perspiration after going only a short distance. And although they sought out the shaded areas and kept to a comfortable pace, Teri had more than once commented that she was certainly going to reform if hell was any hotter than this!

Teri was a tall, slim blond woman. Her fair Nordic coloring belied her Greek ancestry. Also twenty-six, she worked for a petroleum company as an oil and gas land-lease man. She claimed she couldn't yet be a "woman" or a "person" because females constituted only four and one half percent of the profession. "But my time is comin', Ms. Alexander. You just wait and see," she would drawl while she gasped for breath to keep up with her shorter and stronger running mate.

Savvy admired Teri's lean frame. Actually she almost envied her. She knew she would never attain such svelte lines. Savvy had spent most of her life building muscles. She was an athlete and, though she considered herself of amateur status, she could beat the shorts off most men who challenged her to a game of "cutthroat" racquetball. She was good and she knew it, but she never rested on her laurels and continued to lift weights to keep her attractive body strong and firm.

Through it all, Teri constantly assured her that she was the most womanly woman she had ever known. "You're comfortable inside that nice body of yours," she'd declare. "Who could ask for more?"

Savvy did love competition. Wasn't that why she'd decided to go into business for herself? Entertaining and planning the festive decor for public and private functions was paying off, and after only six months. Because she couldn't yet afford extensive paid advertising, she was grateful for her clients' enthusiastic praise, which led to word-of-mouth recommendations. She never regretted her decision; she didn't have the time. She was too busy filling a need in the community.

Her mind seemed constantly occupied with logistical problems for the next assignment or lists of supplies needed for Mr. Goldblum. Her terrifying experience in his building's elevator had prompted a return to their old way of doing business. She would climb the stairs to his sixth-floor office, place her order, then skip back down the steps to await his arrival in the elevator with her supplies. He didn't mind, he assured her. He understood. And Savvy continued to bless his dear, compassionate heart.

Although she was continually busy, the image of Skylar Brady was never far from her thoughts. Often, without consciously recalling the events of that terrible day, Sky's beaming countenance would pop into her head. Sometimes she would smile dreamily at his illusory visage; other times she would blush with the embarrassment she still felt. She didn't think he was devastatingly handsome. "He's more like knock-'em-dead cute!" she'd tell herself. Almost like a full-grown leprechaun. And why not? He's got to be Irish with a name like Brady."

Then she would give herself a hard shake and push the image from her mind. It never stayed away for long, though. His impish dimpled grin was ever ready to bubble to the surface of her consciousness. She truly didn't want to think about him, or what had happened while she was trapped with him. But he kept haunting her thoughts. "Darn it! Get lost, *Skylar*," she'd say. Then she would chuckle when she remembered his words of warning: "And everyone *better* call me Sky!"

Sky on the other hand welcomed his continuing thoughts about Savvy. He had talked with Mr. Goldblum the next day and found out her full name and where she lived. And he hadn't missed the little matchmaker sparks dancing in his friend's lively blue eyes. Nevertheless Sky had asked Mr. Goldblum not to mention his interest to Savvy. Beaming happily, the elderly gentleman had been quick to give his word. He loved being a party to Sky's investigation. "My lips are sealed."

Sky was delighted to discover that Savvy lived in his district and only about a mile from his home. Therefore it was very easy for him to drive by her apartment complex at least once during his work shift as a detective for Tulsa's Finest. Her schedule was anything but routine. Sometimes he would spot her cumbersome purple van parked on the lot, sticking out like a bruised thumb among the well-cared-for cars of her neighbors. Many times it would not be there. Four times in as many weeks he actually saw Savvy climb from her van, but he was never fortunate enough to see her without her clown regalia. When he muttered darkly about his rotten luck, his partner enthusiastically continued his good-natured ribbing.

"She's probably so ugly she never goes out without her clown face, Brady!"

Sky chuckled in reply. "Listen, Connelly, she's got a body that would stop a St. Patrick's Day parade, so why wouldn't she have a face to go along with it?" He could talk to Jake Connelly. They were partners.

Sharing life-and-death situations in their line of work, they also shared a camaraderie that precluded any thought of leaking personal information to others on the force. They trusted one another with their lives; they trusted one another with their secrets. It all went together.

"Why the hell don't you just march yourself up to her door and ask her out, Brady? Now doesn't that make sense?"

"You don't know how I wish I could, buddy. But I don't think she'd be particularly happy to see my ugly puss."

"What'd you do to her in that elevator? I can't picture you taking advantage of a scared woman. That's not your style."

Sky was relieved to know his partner still believed he was a man of integrity. In the past, some of his legendary escapades had threatened to tarnish that image, but above all else, he *was* a man of honor. "You're right, Connelly. That's not my style, but she was so terrified that her recollection is twisted up with her fear. She never wants to see me again."

He sighed in exasperation. What the hell was he going to do about his driving compulsion to know her better? His feelings of frustration were alien to his nature. Basically he was a take-charge guy. And wasn't that exactly what had gotten him into this dilemma in the first place?

Sensing Sky's agitation, Connelly tried to razz him back to normal. He jabbed Sky lightly on his hard, tensed shoulder. Connelly's huge fist could easily knock a man out cold. It went along with the rest of his burly body. He was a bear of a man with craggy, lined features that had seen many tragedies. But the feathery crinkles around his dark eyes also revealed that he knew how to laugh and to enjoy life to the fullest.

"Brady, you're acting like a hound dog in heat! If you don't stop squirming around over there, I'm gonna have to drop you off at your place on our lunch hour so you can swim it off in your pool. And I'll have to make an unannounced midday visit to my ever-lovin' Maggie." His laugh was more like a growl than a chuckle. "Damn, that's not a bad idea anyway," he added decisively.

Sky grabbed a cigarette from the week-old pack on the dash. Although he was determined to stop the filthy habit, he realized he had smoked more this month than he had in the last three. Determinedly he exhaled slowly and tried to relax. "Doesn't that sweet wife of yours ever get tired of your attention?" he bantered disrespectfully. "You've got four kids already, you sex maniac. She must be exhausted."

"She's the best thing that ever happened to me, partner, and you know it. God knows why, but she loves me." Then Connelly laughed with relish, a devilish leer creasing his lined face. "And since we finally discovered what was causing the rash of pregnancies, we don't have to worry about the side effects anymore."

"It took you long enough, genius. I could have straightened you out years ago."

"You mean to tell me *you* knew the reason?" His wide-eyed look of studied innocence sent Sky into a fit of choking laughter and he tossed his cigarette away.

Later that same afternoon Savvy pulled her van into her parking space. She was just getting out with several extra-large balloons when she was greeted by another tenant in her apartment complex.

"Yoo hoo! Savena, dear. How are you this fine day?"

Savvy waved to the small white-haired woman coming toward her and wondered in silent awe how Mrs. Montworthy could look so serene and cool. Probably she used secret potions like rose water and drank mint juleps by the gallon, Savvy decided. Mrs. Montworthy was a Southern lady who never seemed to get flustered by anything.

"I'm very hot, my friend," Savvy answered honestly. "How in the world do you do it?"

The older woman smiled drolly and smoothed a silver curl from her unwrinkled cheek. "Well, my dear. For one thing, I don't go around wearing heavy clown makeup."

"You're not even perspiring, not even a little!"

"Southern ladies are not allowed to perspire, Savena. It's been bred out of our genes."

"I love you," Savvy replied, almost convinced she was telling the truth.

Mrs. Montworthy patted Savvy's hand companionably. It was her way of returning the message. "Why don't you let me treat you to a frosty glass of iced tea at the corner deli, darlin'. I declare, you look absolutely limp. I just cashed my Social Security check and I'm feeling rather extravagant."

Savvy knew her friend lived on a fixed income. She didn't want her to waste her money, but she also didn't want to hurt the woman's feelings. Everyone had to have some pride. "I'd be delighted, dear lady.

But I'll have to run upstairs and clean up first. Do you mind? I can be ready in ten minutes. Come inside with me where it's cool."

Mrs. Montworthy shook her head and the silvery curl fell back across her smooth cheek. "I'll just wait for you here, my dear. This bench in the shade will be just lovely. But if I had a balloon to keep me company, the time would go faster." Her china-blue eyes lit up with childlike mirth as she gazed at Savvy's dancing chorus of floating spheres.

"And of course you'll choose red?"

"You know I always do, Savena," she answered softly. Anchoring the gold twine securely around her fingers, Mrs. Montworthy pulled the string this way and that, totally absorbed in her fascinating plaything. "You run along now. I'll wait right here."

Savvy hurried toward her apartment. In her wake, a balloon trio—blue, yellow, and pink—followed docilely. She hadn't gone ten steps when she heard a strangled cry behind her. Spinning around, she saw her friend being pushed roughly back onto the bench by a mean-looking youth.

"Mrs. Montworthy!" she screamed, running back to her side. "Are you all right?"

"That boy . . . he stole my purse," the pale woman gasped. Her tear-filled eyes were wide with fright. "My money. Savena, he *stole my money!*"

Convinced that her friend was not physically harmed, Savvy let loose her frighting spirit. "I'll get it, Mrs. Montworthy. You stay right here." With that firm promise, she turned and sprinted after the boy. He had a head start, but he had stumbled and fallen over the bushes in his haste to get away, and Savvy took advantage of his error. With her hands in tight, angry fists, the three balloons continued to follow her.

"Stop, thief! Stop!" she bellowed, but the boy didn't hesitate for a second. She had to stop him, Savvy told herself. Mrs. Montworthy's money was in that purse.

As she pushed herself to her limits, she was suddenly struck with a crazy idea. It was just bizarre enough to work . . . provided the kid was as scared as he looked. Not missing a stride in her all-out effort to catch him, she pulled the balloons to her side. "Stop or I'll shoot!" she yelled. When he continued running, she scraped her small diamond ring—her birthstone—across the rigid wall of one large balloon and was rewarded with a resounding bang. Her eyes remained glued to the boy's back. Did he falter in his step? Yes! Quickly she punctured the other two balloons, at the same time shouting, "Hit the pavement!"

Confounded by the shotlike report and her strident order, not to mention the paralyzing fear of bartering his life for one month's pension money, the youth fell to the sidewalk on his belly. "Don't shoot. Don't shoot," he hollered. "I give up."

The young thief surrendered right in front of the deli and Papa Delgadio came bustling out with his trusty shotgun. After being robbed three times, he had sworn he wouldn't ever be robbed again. His twelve-gauge was never far from his side. "Just stay where you are," he ordered gruffly. "You're not going anywhere."

Coming on the scene, Savvy promptly sat herself down in the middle of the boy's back. He was spread face down on the sidewalk, his hands above his head. "You bet you're not going anyplace, you little snot!" She was shaking with anger at his audacity. "Stealing from nice old ladies. You should be ashamed of yourself."

Papa Delgadio's shotgun never wavered from its target. Over his shoulder he called to his wife. "Mama, get the police."

Sky and Connelly heard the call on their radio. They were only half a mile away. "Let's see if we can help," said Sky. "That's Papa's Deli." Three blocks away, they heard a second call.

"We got a purse snatcher. He was captured by a clown!" Hearty laughter filled the airwaves.

"*A clown!*" The exclamation burst from Sky like an expletive. "If that's Savvy, I'll wring her neck. Come on, man, move this bucket of bolts." In moments, they careened around the corner and screeched to a stop in front of the store. Savvy was just getting up off the thief's back when the two leaped from their car.

Through the crowd of people, Sky could hear her excited voice. "*Now* I'll get off, officer. I just wanted to make sure that kid wasn't going anyplace until you got the handcuffs on him."

Taking a deep breath and bracing himself for whatever Savvy might say to him, Sky shouldered his way through the crowd until he was face-to-face with his mental nemesis. "Well, if it isn't the Balloon Girl," he observed calmly. His heart, however, was beating like a jackhammer.

Without looking up, Savvy tensed. That voice! No, it couldn't be. Pulling flippancy around her like a cloak of security, she muttered belligerently. "If you must call me names, Balloon *Woman* would be more appropriate."

"Don't you think I know that?" His quiet retort brought her head up with a comical jerk.

"Mr. Brady! It *is* you. I didn't recognize you with your clothes on." Instantly she realized her faux pas and tried to correct herself for the interested audience. "Oh, no! I didn't mean that like it sounded . . . I . . . I . . ." He just stood there, grinning, watching her dig her own grave. "Darn it, Brady," she exploded. "You know what I mean."

"Certainly, Ms. Alexander, but do these other folks?"

"I've got to check on Mrs. Montworthy," she snapped, exasperated, turning to push her way out of the circle of chuckling observers. "Please let me through." She was feeling trapped again; the tightness in her throat was threatening to cut off her air supply. "Please!" She gasped frantically.

At once Sky saw the look of terror glaze her wide eyes and used his own body to make a pathway for her. "Come on, Savvy. This way."

When she was free of the spectators she ran back to her friend, who was still seated on the bench. The woman's only outward sign of distress was the swooning manner in which she fanned herself with a snowy, lace-edged handkerchief. "Mrs. Montworthy, are you feeling all right? We got your money back. Everything is under control again." She was not aware that Sky had followed her and was standing right behind her with his arms folded across his chest.

The older woman, however, gazed in amazement

over Savvy's shoulder at his steely eyes and grim expression. "My dear Savena. I'm so grateful you weren't hurt, darlin'. And it's wonderful you savin' my money and all. It was a very brave thing for you to do. But, my dear, I don't think everything is under control . . . yet." Her eyes danced merrily and she added in a ladylike, hushed whisper. "Have you looked at your escort's face? I believe you're about to get a lecture about derring-do."

Savvy sliced a glance behind her and was chilled by Sky's riveting glare of reproach. Her stomach convulsed nervously, but she obstinately refused to show her fear. She would tough it out . . . as usual. "He hasn't got any say over me, Mrs. Montworthy."

Although Sky wanted to paddle the rounded posterior of his sharp-tongued adversary, he controlled himself. Instead, his stern mouth smoothed into a congenial smile when he turned toward the older woman. Bending low to take her frail hand in his, he spoke courteously. "I'm very happy to meet you, ma'am. And may I say I am extremely grateful such a fine lady as you has escaped unharmed after your distressing experience. I'd like to introduce myself, Mrs. Montworthy. My name is Skylar Brady. Detective Brady. But please feel free to call me Sky."

Before the woman could gather her charmed senses to reply, Savvy ungraciously retorted, "You're a cop?"

"*Detective*, Ms. Alexander," he corrected. "Why are you so surprised? Most men wouldn't feel obligated to climb down an elevator shaft to rescue a crazy female in a clown suit!" He hoped that condescending statement would shut her up, but he was mistaken. She was sputtering for control, trying to find words scathing enough to serve her purpose, so he put an iron grip on her arm and apologized to her friend, who was watching with undisguised interest. "Please excuse us, ma'am. Ms. Alexander has to answer quite a few questions for our arrest report."

With a serene smile and a slight wave of her lace handkerchief, Mrs. Montworthy dismissed them and Sky marched Savvy over to the far side of her van. He effortlessly turned around her stiff, uncooperative body, then he leaned forward to hiss into her painted funnyface, "Now, Savvy. What the hell did you think you were doing? You little fool! You could have gotten yourself killed." Unconsciously he was shaking her back and forth inside her baggy clown suit.

Fighting mad again, Savvy snapped back at him, "If you don't stop shaking me, I'm going to start screaming, 'Police brutality!' " Her pointed message sank into his churning brain and he dropped his hands with a gruff apology.

Before either of them could say another word, Connelly came striding over. "Did she tell you what she did? Damn fool thing, but it worked. I'd a never believed it, but that punk was scared sh— I mean, spitless."

His face a deathly white, Sky turned to his partner. "No, Jake, Ms. Alexander hasn't enlightened me. Suppose you fill me in on the *exciting* details."

Connelly realized he was witnessing the calm before the storm and felt sorry for Savvy. She was going to get a royal chewing out! But she had it coming, he told himself. It would be for her own good. But, damn, he had to admire the woman's spunk.

"She captured the kid all by herself. Ran after him when he grabbed the lady's purse. But what's really funny is how she got him to surrender. Are you ready for this, Brady? She popped balloons and made him think it was pistol shots. Boy, that's rich!" He chuckled for a moment, then straightened up and made his exit, muttering beneath his breath, "Damn fool thing to do, though."

Sky was almost speechless with rage. He turned his cold steel blue eyes back on Savvy. "You *popped balloons* at him?" he asked, incredulously. "What would you have done if he'd shot back . . . with real bullets?" His sharp words cut deep.

"He didn't have a chance. Papa was there with his shotgun." Savvy was beginning to feel the shock of what she had done, but she couldn't let Sky see how she was reacting.

"And what would you have done if Papa hadn't come out with his gun? Beat the thief over the head with your fright wig?"

"I sat on him," she croaked defensively. "He wasn't going anywhere." She had a difficult time meeting his level, disbelieving glare, but she forced herself to keep staring back into his icy blue eyes. Irrationally she decided she liked his face better when he was smiling like a leprechaun, and the image that popped up made a nervous giggle slip out as well.

Her irreverent snicker snapped Sky into action. Without a word he grabbed her arm and escorted her briskly to the police officers who were getting ready to put their prisoner into a squad car. "Just a minute, Officer Dodd. I'd like a word with the suspect if you don't mind." The policeman shrugged and told Sky to take his time.

Sky gave the young thief a deadly look. "Well, Jocko, we meet again," he said. The tall boy only smirked cockily. Sky took a menacing step toward him and the boy shrank back, his show of bravado erased. "I thought I told you I never wanted to catch you in my district," Sky said harshly. "I thought I made it clear you weren't to set foot on my turf unless you had a personal engraved invitation from me. Now what do I find? You're here, stealing from defenseless old ladies." He spoke as if his words were bullets, aimed directly at the boy. "Well, I'm finished with you, Jocko. This time we're going to put you away. You've pulled your last job in my part of Tulsa."

He took a deep, disgusted breath and turned to Savvy. "This subhuman is Jocko, Ms. Alexander. What do you think?"

"He's just a kid," she whispered imploringly. Sky would have bet a month's wages that he would see that look in her eyes. She was feeling sorry for this punk!

Sky gave her a sharp look and said, "On the streets, he's known as Jocko the Blade. Would you care to see why?"

He took her silence for assent and asked the officer for any weapons he'd found on the boy. The policeman tossed an evidence bag to Sky, who caught it easily. He turned it upside down over his opened hand and a metallic object dropped out. Seemingly without Sky moving, the object snapped to attention in his hand. It was a ten-inch switchblade knife! "Jocko never travels anywhere without it," he confided in a low, ominous voice. Savvy's gasp of realization drove him to make his point, once and for all. "If Papa hadn't come out when he did, Jocko would have carved you up like a Christmas goose . . . and he wouldn't have blinked an eye. *Do I make myself clear?*"

She nodded and great tears began to spill from her frightened eyes, creating a stark contrast with her painted red smile. "Perfectly clear, Detective Brady," she whispered. "I could have been killed."

"Exactly." He returned the knife to the bag and handed it over to the arresting officer. "Take this scum to the station, Steve. He's all yours." Sky glanced at his watch and realized his duty was over for the day. Spotting Jake, he asked him to sign out for him. "I'll see that Ms. Alexander comes down to the station within the hour. I suspect she'll want to change into other clothes and clean up first."

Connelly silently gave him a jaunty salute, but his eyes were saying, You old reprobate, Brady. You're gonna get a look at that face if it's the last thing you do! Sky's guarded wink told him he was right.

"Shall we, Ms. Alexander?" he suggested, taking her firmly in hand and leading her back to her apartment building. Though his words were polite, the edge of command in his tone did not encourage Savvy to disobey. She walked docilely by his side, once again very consicous of his tall, muscular build. Even though he was fully clothed, she was still aware of the breadth of his shoulders and wondered if his suit had been tailor-made, it fit his well-developed biceps and tapered torso so well. He seemed taller, she thought. Then the steady click of his heels drew her downcast eyes to his lizard-skin boots and she knew why. She could tell he took some pride in his appearance; only men who knew they had good bodies would wear trousers molding their thighs like Sky's did. Moaning softly, she wished they had met under different circumstances. A game of cutthroat racquetball would be a peak experience!

He glanced down at her when he heard her low sigh. "You're not going to faint on me, are you, Savvy?" Was there just the least bit of tenderness in his voice?

She shook her head and kept on walking. "No, I just think I'm feeling after-shock. In retrospect, I did a very foolish thing."

"That's the first smart thing I've heard from you today," he agreed grimly, holding her arm a little more firmly as they ascended the steps to her second-floor apartment. "Where's your key?"

Self-consciously she thrust her fingers into the top of the clown suit and fished around until she found the ribbon around her neck. "Here," she answered weakly, beginning to tremble all over.

He slipped the key over her head and unlocked the door. "You're the oldest latchkey child I've ever met," he muttered, pushing the door open for her.

"I can't carry a purse when I'm working," she explained in a small voice. Then she collapsed into the corner of the cocoa velour sofa and began to shake in earnest.

Immediately Sky was all business. "Do you have any liquor? You're going to be a basket case if I don't find you a stiff drink." He followed her vague hand signal to the kitchen and began to throw open cabinets and a small pantry in his frantic search. "Pay dirt," he exclaimed triumphantly, unbending himself from the lower corner cabinet with a bottle of brandy in his hand. He grabbed a water glass from a shelf and splashed a hefty measure of brandy into it while he hurried to her side. "Here, kid. Drink this down." Again his words left no room for argument. Savvy drained the glass in three swallows and then gasped for breath from the potent fire she'd thrown down her throat. He chuckled in satisfaction. "That should get your circulation moving."

"Or knock me out cold!" Surprisingly, she didn't feel light-headed and after a few minutes her nerves settled down. She lifted her head and met Sky's concerned gaze.

"Better?"

"Mmm, thanks."

"If you didn't have on your whiteface, I'd be able to tell if the color were coming back into your cheeks," he teased softly. "But I can see your eyes have lost that shocked glaze. I think you'll survive your derring-do, as Mrs. Montworthy so aptly described it." Suddenly he felt glad to be with her, clown suit and all. She was a paradox, he decided. Terrified of some things and fearless of others . . . at least until they were over.

He reached down and took her icy hands in his warm grasp, easing her to her feet. "Do you feel up to taking a hot shower, Savvy? I think you'll need that before you come fully back to life." He continued to gaze at her smeared funnyface, thinking she was the saddest-looking clown in the world. "Your makeup is all tear-streaked and melted again," he whispered, gently removing her blazing fright wig. Underneath he found a nylon cap holding her own hair snug and out of sight. "May I?" Without waiting for her permission, he tugged off the covering and grinned in unabashed delight when a mane of champagne curls tumbled into his hands. "Now, that's a step in the right direction," he murmured approvingly, fingering the silken strands. When she lifted a bright blue diamond-shaped eyebrow in question, he added, "At least you're not bald!"

She laughed and felt better for it. "You say the sweetest things, Detective Brady."

"Hey, don't knock it, lady. I've been wandering around my district for four weeks trying to get a look at you." He realized his error too late. Damn you and your big mouth, he fumed silently.

By this time, though, Savvy had gathered her senses and heard every word. "Which reminds me," she said suspiciously, "you called me Ms. Alexander." Was he actually beginning to blush? What did he have to be embarrassed about? *She* was the lunatic!

"That's your name, isn't it?" Her faint accusation had put him on the defensive.

"Yes, but you didn't know it . . . and how did you know I lived in this apartment?"

"Mr. Goldblum," he admitted, grudgingly. "I spoke to him the day after we met. I was worried about you . . . and I wanted to get to know you better." There, he felt relieved for having finally admitted his interest in her.

But his words cut deep into her shame. She jerked her hands from his and angrily pulled open the front door. Anger was all she had left. He certainly didn't leave her with a shred of dignity. "We may not know each other in the biblical sense of the word, but I think we know each other in terms of character and personality as well as we ever will. You'd better leave, Detective Brady. I'll find my own way to the station."

His face was grim when he reached behind her and slammed the door shut with a resounding bang. "Stop it, Savvy!" He took her shoulders in his large hands. His eyes were blazing and a muscle jumped in his clenched jaw. "I told you then and I'll tell you now, *forget it*! You were terrified beyond reason. I know that. If you'll give yourself a little sympathy you'll admit it too. I never *ever* thought you were some quick trick, easy to make and easier to discard." His words were brutal, but he had to make himself clear. "I *do* want to know you better. I want to see your face. Is that so much to ask? All I know is that you have the biggest, most expressive green eyes in the world." *And your mouth is as soft as rose petals under mine,* he added silently. His tone softened, too, when he asked, "Well? What about it, Savvy?"

"No!"

Doggedly he refused to accept her one-syllable answer. "Where's your courage now?"

A tiny flicker of a smile tugged at the corner of her red-painted mouth. "Lying in a shallow grave some-where between here and Papa's Deli."

He grinned in relief. She was going to let him stay. He could feel it in his bones. "Why don't you get ready? I'll wait out on your balcony. Okay?"

"Okay," she answered softly, silently thanking him for his considerate thought. A rough-edged diamond he might be, but his gruff demeanor shielded a gallant man, she decided. "I'll be ready in half an hour." Without another word, she walked across the forest green carpet to her bathroom.

Sky was alone, and he took the time to survey her home. The living room, dining area, and kitchen formed an L-shape. Sparkling white with dark wood cabinetry, the galley kitchen was designed for efficient movement. On the walls were embroidered rattan baskets and a large mirror with a stained-glass motif. The dining nook held an oak table and four chairs. A shrimp-colored cloth with matching candles in wooden holders graced the sturdy rectangle. At two places tan raffia mats with contrasting napkins were set. *Two?* He gasped in bewilderment. Did she live with someone? Someone *male?* Damn, he'd never even thought about that. He had a real penchant for overlooking the competition. Only this time, it definitely mattered. Just cool it, Brady, he warned himself. Don't jump to conclusions. Wait and ask later . . . *casually.*

He strolled back into the living room. The stark white walls were a perfect background for a large numbered iris print over the glass-doored fireplace in the corner and a surrealistic gold sculpture over the couch that on closer inspection revealed itself to be a flock of seagulls. He smiled when he glanced back at the gold-framed flower. Purple again! Directly opposite the dark brown sofa, a more than adequate stereo system with large speakers was positioned on a natural oak table. Next to it was a brown tubular chair and footrest cushioned in coffee-colored sailcloth, and a good reading lamp. Falling back on his investigative training, Sky was able to deduce that Savvy took pride in her home, but she also lived in it. A stack of books and another of magazines provided evidence for his theory. Altogether, she valued her comfortable surroundings, he decided.

Hearing the shower stop, he made his exit onto the tiny wooden balcony and settled himself into a folding chair. He refused to think past the present moment while he sat quietly, watching the world go by on the sidewalk and parking lot beyond.

Savvy opened the bathroom door a crack, allowing a cloud of steam to escape. Although she was covered from head to toe in a thick terry robe and a towel turban, she wanted to make sure Sky was keeping his word. Leaning out into the hallway, she saw him on her little porch. He was sitting in her one lawn chair, his back to the door. Scurrying like a frightened rabbit, she crossed into her bedroom and shut and locked the door.

Well, genius, he's still here, she lamented. All that wishing while you were under the shower didn't do a bit of good. She knew he wouldn't disappear. He had his duty to perform. She had to go to the police station to make a statement, maybe even identify that little thief in a lineup.

The prospect of this new experience piqued her curiosity and she quickly began to dress. Since this was strictly a business appointment she should probably wear a suit, but it was so hot outside. She had been close to heat stroke all day in her clown costume. She just had to go for cool this evening . . . in more ways than one! she cautioned, refusing to believe Sky's impassioned speech. He probably had all the girlfriends he could handle. He certainly didn't need to chase another one in a clown suit. Still, he seemed sincere, she mused, vacillating in her decision like the pendulum in a cuckoo clock. An apt metaphor, she decided, pulling a demure lavender-flowered sundress over her panties and slip.

Her tanned skin glowed as she stood before her mirror in the slanted sunbeams that poured through her bedroom window. She smoothed a fragrant lotion over her bare shoulders, arms, and legs before she stepped into her high-heeled strap sandals.

Leaning over, she towel dried her long blond hair and slipped back into the bathroom to blow dry it into a shimmering halo of pale curls. She applied her makeup carefully. After all, she reminded herself, Detective Brady said he was waiting to see her face. She enhanced her already large jade eyes with under-stated emerald shadow, liner, and mink mascara. A touch of plum blush on her cheeks and a matching shade of lip gloss completed the job. Retracing her steps, she checked the contents of her white leather clutch bag and misted her pulse points with a subtle musky fragrance.

Glancing one last time into the full-length mirror, she knew it was time to meet Sky without her funnyface. Lord, if he made one crack about her forgetting to take off the clown mask, she'd deck him! Firmly she told herself to have a little confidence.

She took a deep breath and walked quietly into the living room. Sky was still seated where she had last seen him. The patio doors were opened wide and a gentle breeze played at the sheer white curtain drawn to one side. She nervously cleared her throat.

"I'm ready, Sky."

He rose instantly and walked across the carpeted room. He stood before her for long moments, until Savvy's skin began to crawl. The look on his face was something between shocked pleasure and disbelief. Her nerves were stretched to the breaking point. If he didn't say something soon, she knew she was going to scream!

"I knew it," he murmured in wonder. "I knew you'd . . . be lovely." He stopped his words just in time. If he had repeated his earlier statement to Connelly about knowing she'd have a face to go along with her body, he'd be back in hot water again. "What a shame you have to keep yourself all covered up for your job."

"I don't have to be in costume all the time," she said, smiling in relief that he seemed to like what he saw. "That's only part of my work. And it's my own business," she corrected proudly. "I also design and provide decorations for private banquets and meetings. They don't like clowns clowning around at business functions, but they seem to enjoy balloons in the decor. Makes them think about rising sales and high profits." She laughed, embarrassed. "I'm gushing," she apologized. "I always get carried away when I'm talking business."

He wondered if that was the only time she got carried away? That and in stuck elevators. But he kept these thoughts—or could they be wishes?—to himself. "I'm sure you're very successful," he replied. "Does your business have a name?"

"The Light Side."

He tried to consider her answer but had a difficult time even listening to her words. She was more beautiful than he'd ever imagined she might be. "The Light Side. An appropriate name for a ballooning business."

"I'm glad you approve," she said, giggling at his pun.

"Ms. Alexander, I approve of everything about you." He leaned closer. "Mmmm, your perfume is wonderful." Clearing his throat, he straightened his tie and tried to look serious. "I think we'd better get out of here. We've got a lot of paperwork to wade through before dinner." He shut and locked the glass door, then pulled the curtains closed.

Savvy felt a rush of pleasure at his first comment and a chill of apprehension at his assumption about dinner. "Will it take that long to get this report filled out? I really wasn't planning on having dinner with you."

His eyes narrowed as he turned back to her. "Why not? Have you got another date? Or a business appointment?" When she shook her head, he began to breathe again. "Well, Savvy, we're going to have dinner . . . together . . . tonight. You've got a whole lot of explaining to do."

"*I do not!*"

"Wanna bet, baby?" And speechless, Savvy was led down the stairs.

Three

The heat was still oppressive and Savvy dreaded the ride in her old van. It had no air conditioning. She'd look like a wilted lettuce leaf in fifteen minutes, she thought drearily. But Sky led her instead to a low-slung silver sports car parked next to her van. Deftly he unlocked the door and helped her in.

"Is taking joy rides a side venture for you?" she asked, wondering where the unfamiliar car had come from.

"It belongs to me, Savvy. I'm a good cop, remember?" He grinned at her embarrassed expression. "Jake, my partner, brought it over for me. He knew

I'd be needing it because I wouldn't want to take you out in your old clunker."

"Violet gives me very good service," she retorted contrarily, although she knew she'd enjoy riding in cool comfort for a change. "And how did he know? You didn't ask him to bring it."

"He knows *me!*" With that cryptic statement Sky closed the door, walked around the car, and slid behind the steering wheel. In a short time they were driving along the busy streets to the police station. Savvy had to admit she admired the power of the car and the expert way in which Sky handled it.

It took less than an hour to give her statement and answer the questions for the case officer. She was a little disappointed when she found out she wouldn't have to identify Jocko in a lineup. Sky explained that it wasn't necessary because he had been arrested at the scene of the crime. "Thanks to your hare-brained courage!"

"And Papa's shotgun!" He refused to argue with her and silently ushered her back to his car. His unspoken inference that she could have been badly hurt or worse because of her unthinking action upset her. When they were driving again, Savvy felt more and more uncomfortable. If this was going to continue, she didn't want to spend the evening with Sky.

"Look," she said, "I think you'd better just take me home. You've done your job and I can see this is going to turn into a miserable evening. We're going to argue about everything."

He allowed only a swift assessing glance at her serious eyes before he turned his gaze back to the road. His words softly broke the unsettled stillness. "That's where I'm taking you . . . home." He checked his thin gold wristwatch. "Hooker should have dinner ready when we get there."

"Hooker?"

Sky chuckled dangerously. He had read every insinuating inflection in her one-word question. "Not *that* kinda hooker, Savvy. I'm surprised at you. Hooker is an old friend."

"Male or female?" She bit her tongue, but too late. You had to ask, didn't you? she scolded in disgust.

"Definitely male. And he enjoys using black humor, so don't let him throw you."

"Black humor?"

He laughed at her question this time. "Not racist barbs, you little nut. Black as in turned-toward-oneself jokes. He makes fun of himself before anyone else has a chance."

Savvy tried hard to keep up with Sky's explanation, but it was almost impossible. Here they were, driving along toward his house, talking about one of his friends and her nerves were going haywire. He had warned her. She would have to explain many things this evening. What in the world would he want to know? Would he question her about her behavior in the elevator? Well, she didn't want to talk to him about that. No way! All she wanted was to forget how she had met him, and the embarrassing way she had acted.

Pulling herself back to the present, she tried to concentrate on the conversation. "Why does your friend make fun of himself? Does he have two heads or something?"

"No," he answered wickedly. "He's a model."

His words uncorked her impish sense of humor. How could she keep her distance from him when he kept tickling her funnybone? Moaning, she covered her flushed cheeks with her hands, chuckling silently. "Oh?"

"Well, get it out of your system now, kid, because Hooker will have a field day if you make any snide remarks in front of him, you know?"

"I know."

Sky's guarded glance told Savvy he knew exactly what he had said. He was subtly reminding her of her flippancy and the tough outer shell that she used to protect herself in uncomfortable situations. She wondered how he defended himself.

"We grew up together and fought in one of those foreign police actions," he explained, his smile disappearing. "Police action!" He snorted in disgust. "That's a hell of a euphemism for a small war in another country. One night on patrol our squad was caught in an ambush and Hooker was wounded. We've been really close ever since."

Her words trembled on her lips when she spoke. She wasn't sure she wanted to hear his answer to her question. "Were you hurt?"

"Not so you'd notice. Some scars don't show." But his grim expression revealed some fierce residual effect from that awful experience. Suddenly he was vulnerable . . . and it touched Savvy's heart.

She couldn't help herself. She lifted her fingers and traced the straight tightness of his usually warm and mobile mouth. Her tender gesture surprised Sky. He caught her hand in his and turned to look keenly at her brimming emerald eyes. Her lashes were separated into tiny star points. His heart did a little double beat when he saw her tear-filled, shining gaze. She was hurting for him, he thought in wonder. His voice dropped with the emotions he was feeling. "Maybe someday I'll be able to tell you about it, but not now. All right?"

Savvy nodded in acceptance and they continued the drive through the twilight, still holding hands, both lost in their own thoughts. When he pulled into the driveway of his home, she was recalling and accepting as truth Mr. Goldblum's wise words: We all have some secret inner fear.

Sky's home was a big surprise. Literally! He lived in a huge stone mansion built on several wooded acres. When he helped her from the car, he laughed at her gaping mouth. "Welcome home, Savvy."

"You *really* live here?"

"Yup!"

"What are you? A lottery millionaire?"

He grinned into her wide, questioning eyes, then gave her a gentle hug and a little peck on the cheek. "I'm sure glad you didn't accuse me of being a cop on the take." The indignant expression on her face told him that the thought had never occurred to her and he felt good all over. "Come on inside. Hooker's going to be very upset if we're not ready to eat when he's ready to serve. A real temperamental cook, our Hooker."

She followed at his side, gripping his hand as firmly as a child being led into a new, unfamiliar experience. "You didn't answer my question, Sky."

"Later, Savvy. First we eat, then we'll have our talk. And it'll be a two-way conversation, I promise. Okay?"

"Okay." She stood quietly while he unlocked the heavy white front door and escorted her into a large foyer. At once she received the impression of relaxed, comfortable light. The walls were painted a restful pale lemon; the floor reflected the warmth of burnished golden oak parquet. It felt cool, too, and she conservatively wondered what it must cost for utilities. "You have a beautiful home, Sky. It's spacious."

"Yeah, it's big all right. I use it more for a tax shelter at the moment, but someday soon I'm going to begin filling it up with kids."

"I hope that's agreeable with your wife." Why hadn't it occurred to her that he might be engaged or married? Because of the episode in the elevator, that's why! The shock of hearing about his plan tore the mask of friendliness from her face and he saw her inner turmoil.

"I haven't got a wife, nor am I engaged." His words allowed the veil to descend once more but this time Savvy's features were more relaxed. He watched, fascinated, when her expressive eyes began to dance with teasing merriment.

"Someone really should have told you before this, Detective Brady. You can't do *that* job alone."

"Don't you think I know that, woman?" In turn, she watched as his expression changed rapidly from red-faced embarrassment to a scowl of indignation.

She giggled softly. "Just giving you the facts, sir."

Muttering beneath his breath—something about smart-aleck collectors of television trivia—he grabbed her hand and led her toward the back of the house. The fragrant smells wafting toward them indicated they were approaching the kitchen.

"You're about to enter the lair of the consummate jokester, Ms. Alexander. I shall enjoy the ensuing massacre." His gruff words were meant to show the measure of his sadism, but his tender expression told Savvy the real story. He figured if he gave her a hand, she'd make it through her first meeting with Hooker.

Her competitive spirit rose to the surface. "I don't need your help, mister."

"Damn, you're an impudent, contrary woman."

"It's part of my scintillating appeal," she countered, giving him a dazzling smile before entering the kitchen. She was still smiling when a man, as large as Sky but with dark good looks, turned from the sink and grinned at the jaunty interloper. His white slacks and soft shirt were protected by a tomato-red apron that read, Cooks Make Spicy Lovers!

Not waiting for Sky's introduction, Savvy strolled to the man's side and met his steady, measuring gaze. "Hi! I'm Savena Alexander. My friends call me Savvy. Wanna be friends, Hooker?" Her insides were busy knitting themselves into an afghan square, however, because standing before her was the Stallion Man—one of her favorite commercials. Sexy, sexy, sexy!

The man didn't flicker an eyelash at Savvy's question. "The full name's Hooker Jablonski . . . and I wanna be friends with you, Savvy. One thing, though. I don't shake hands with beautiful women. I hug!" With that declaration, he gathered her against him in a heart-stopping embrace. Setting her gently back on her feet, he confirmed his first statement. "I'm very glad to meet you, Savvy."

He stood ready to catch her. Swooning women were

an occupational hazard for him. But although he could see the spark of recognition in her emerald eyes, he could also see she was going to keep it in check, and his respect and interest in her grew dramatically. He sliced a wicked glance at Sky, who was leaning indolently against the counter taking in the action. "You've got yourself a live one, Brady."

"I'll wait a while before I pass judgment," Sky drawled, gazing directly at Savvy. Was there a glint of challenge in his eyes? Why was he goading her? Did he want her to fall on her face? She chose to ignore him.

"Sky told me you're a model," Savvy said, gazing unflinchingly at Hooker's handsome face, not allowing her eyes to give his breathtaking frame the once-over that normally must follow, even when his occupation was not known. "Was it difficult to learn?"

When she continued to meet his steady gaze, she knew he was weighing her words. Was she razzing him or did she really want to know? His wary look changed into a wide smile. Apparently he decided she was really curious. And Savvy knew his perception about her thoughts were correct. Before her stood a *man*—devastatingly handsome—who happened to make his living as a model and television actor.

"Naw!" he answered. "It was easy." As if to add substance to his words he struck a frozen pose, sucked in his cheeks like a mannequin, and snapped his fingers jauntily. "My body works perfectly."

"For which he has the undying appreciation and devotion of his many women friends," interjected Sky with a dirty chuckle.

"Can I help it if I have sex appeal?"

Savvy was not to be outdone by Detective Brady. "I wish you'd add me to that list, Hooker. I admire you very much." He did look like a Greek god with his classic dark features offset by his dazzling white outfit.

"You sure Savvy knows she's supposed to be *your* friend, Brady?" He seemed impervious to Sky's indignant glare.

"I choose my own friends, Hooker," Savvy insisted.

"Not the way *he* wants to be friends," Hooker whispered brazenly. "That isn't what he has in mind at all."

Savvy absolutely refused to blush. She stood staunchly to her full height and whispered back, "We both know he hasn't much of a mind to have anything in!"

Hooker whooped with glee and whirled her around the kitchen in another bear hug, expertly skirting the red-faced third member of their trio. "Lady, I *am* glad to meet you. You might just give ole son here a run for his money."

"I already have."

"She already has."

Both answered at the same time, but Savvy was thinking about the recent capture of the purse snatcher while Sky was reliving time spent in a dark elevator.

"I'm not getting in the middle of *that* one!" Hooker declared. "Wanna see me do my stuff?"

"You're going to pose for me?"

"Heck, no! I'm going to cook for you."

"I thought you already were," she drawled, batting

her eyes. Sky snorted and choked at her sauciness, but Hooker just winked flirtatiously so Savvy continued to play along with him.

"I have to be very careful about dishpan hands," he observed, swishing his fingers delicately through the soapy water in the sink. "They don't photograph well."

"You could lose an Ivory commercial, huh?"

His grin widened. This was going to be a game of one-upmanship. Terrific, he mused happily. He loved to push his jokes to the limit. "I have to be careful using knives for the same reason."

She rolled her eyes and stepped to his side. "Heaven forbid if you'd cut anything *really important* . . . like your dimpled chin," she bantered, tapping her fingertip on the spot.

His look of incredulity made Savvy hesitate. Had she gone too far? "Sky, if you don't take good care of her, I'm going to put in my bid." Hooker's voice was tender, yet carried a warning to his friend, and her unspoken question was answered.

Sky didn't have a chance to answer.

"I'm my own person, Hooker," Savvy said seriously.

"I think Sky and I both know that, little darlin'. You're definitely one of a kind." Hooker's look was almost worshipful.

Sky cleared his throat, getting both Savvy and Hooker's attention. "Would you like to see the rest of the house, Savvy?"

She didn't want to be alone with Sky. Not yet. Maybe never. "Perhaps later, Sky. I'd better help Hooker finish dinner." She turned back to Hooker and pleaded silently for his cooperation. "You could use some help, couldn't you?"

He read her distress signal loud and clear. "I can always use the help of a beautiful woman, Savvy."

"Then I hope you won't be *too* upset if I excuse myself," Sky declared grumpily. "I'd like to clean up before dinner. Rescuing clowns can be hot work!" He heard Savvy inhale sharply as he turned on his heel and walked out of the room, thinking to himself that he was fighting a losing battle. She was afraid of him. She thought all he wanted to do was get her into bed because of that damned elevator incident. Suddenly he stopped in his tracks and chuckled softly. She was right, of course, but all in good time. That straightened out to his satisfaction, he jogged up the steps, whistling happily under his breath.

"Whew!" Hooker said. "That man's got a burr under his saddle and I think it may be you. I've never seen him react to a little kidding like that."

"I don't know why," Savvy answered belligerently, snapping a tea towel around her waist to protect her dress. "All he does is yell at me. I can't help it. When someone pushes me, I usually push back."

"You don't realize how special you are, do you? I saw it the minute you lit up my kitchen. I suspect Sky knows it too. What happened? Did you two get off on the wrong foot or something?"

"Or something," she said sullenly. If Hooker didn't know already, if Sky hadn't told the world about what happened in that elevator, then she certainly wasn't going to explain. She'd die before she ever revealed the circumstances surrounding their first encounter.

Hooker understood he was treading on confidential territory and began to chatter carelessly about other things. Before long both were carrying on a relaxed conversation. Savvy tore spinach for the salad while Hooker whipped up an Italian dressing. A question kept coming into her mind. She had to ask it.

"What happened to Sky after you were wounded?"

Hooker hesitated for an instant as he mixed the dressing, then casually continued. "What did Sky tell you?"

"Just that his scars don't show. What did he mean?"

Hooker fixed her with a faraway look, lost for a time in his own thoughts. Then he shook his head almost imperceptibly and replied, giving no answer at all. "I think you'd better wait until Sky feels ready to tell you himself. I will say that he saved my worthless life. He's a damned hero, but you'll never hear about it from him."

"Is that why you work for him . . . besides modeling?" If he owed Sky his life, perhaps that was the reason. He surely didn't need the money. He was a top model and commercial actor.

Hooker laughed until he had to grab a dish towel to mop his eyes. "Savvy, not even Skylar Brady can afford my culinary skills. I'm priceless, didn't you know?"

She didn't have to be hit on the head to realize the door was closed on her attempted research. Hooker was no gossip, even though she felt certain he knew her interest was genuine. She just hoped Sky valued Hooker's loyal friendship. Then her bright smile reflected in her teasing jade eyes. "Do all your lady friends think you're priceless too?"

"I give 'em my best shot, Savvy," he countered with that wicked leer. "But I could use a bit of advice from an intelligent woman like you."

"I'll be glad to help if I can, Hooker." Her reply was so serious, it was difficult for Hooker to contain himself as he led her right down the garden path.

"Well, the problem is this. How can I tell if they love me for myself . . . or if they only want to get their hands on my secret recipes?"

It was Savvy's turn to stare him down without so much as a blink of her eyes. "Piece of cake, Hooker!" He flinched at her corny choice of words. "You'll know they want your recipes if they wear vanilla extract instead of Chanel Number 5. You may run into a puzzling complication, however." She knew a thing or two about leading down a path. She leaned forward and her voice dropped to a seductive, confidential whisper. "Sometimes both kinds of women like to fool around with whipped cream!"

When Hooker could control his uninhibited response, he said hoarsely, "Brady said you were well named." His face beamed with approval. She had made a new friend.

Savvy was alone in the dining room when Sky came back down the stairs. She saw him before he spotted her. It gave her a moment to appreciate his magnificent physique. Now there was a man! Tall, blond, handsome. Great body, expressive eyes, good sense of humor. But very, very bossy, she decided. And pushy too. What could ever come of a relationship with someone like him? And their first meeting could never be far from his thoughts. She certainly knew it had stayed with her. Her cheeks grew hot at the memory.

It was at that moment, of course, that he should glance up and pin her with his laser blue gaze. She was unable to tear her eyes from his and continued to receive the heat of his unspoken message across the room. He moved toward her with the grace and bearing of a man in control. Had she been able to feel his heart beating like a jungle drum beneath his teal blue shirt, she would have known he was testing the waters . . . trying to ascertain the temperature of her response after his absence.

"You look more comfortable now," she murmured, searching for something to say.

He glanced down at his form-fitting jeans and scuffed boots, then grinned back at her flushed face. "I try not to wear suits unless I'm working or out on the town. I'm really a country boy at heart. And for me, these are what I call friendly clothes."

"I feel the same way about my clown costume as you do about business suits," she replied, finally over her initial shyness at being alone with him. "Hooker said he'll be right back."

"What did you think of him?"

"I think you have a wonderful friend, Sky. I hope he can be mine too."

"After watching you two in action, I can almost guarantee you've made a friend for life." He lifted his hand to her hair and played bemusedly with a fallen curl that insisted on winding around his index finger. "I wonder how it would feel?"

When he stood so close she always had difficulty thinking. This was no exception. "What would?"

"Having you as a friend for life." He continued to trace her curls and outline her features, ending with a whisper touch on her full lower lip. His eyes had changed again from steel blue to an indigo shade. She could feel herself falling into their depths and floating there, suspended in the universe of his mind.

Suddenly she knew he was going to kiss her. She drew away from his touch and walked to the other side of the small table near the window. She stood gazing out with unseeing eyes over the wooded landscape. "Friendships take time and attention," she said, playing for time because her mind refused to work.

He followed her and stood quietly behind her stiff, unyielding body. His whispered breath tantalized her senses. "We're connected . . . for life, Savvy. I saved yours. That makes me responsible for the rest of it."

She spun around and faced him. "You didn't save my life," she argued. "I wasn't in any real danger. I was just trapped and frightened."

"Then I saved your sanity."

She nodded solemnly and bowed her head. "Yes, you did that. And I'm still embarrassed even to think about it," she said softly. "I must have completely flipped, but I was so frightened. I haven't been able to go into closed places for years."

He gently enfolded her in his arms, willing her to relax against him. It wasn't difficult for her to do. "You were almost out of your mind with fear, honey," he said tenderly. "I know that. But I meant what I said to you after it was over. I *do* want to know you."

His last words caused her to raise her head and he leaned against her, touching foreheads, and closed his eyes. "I saved your sanity and I've been losing mine for the past month trying to find a way to see you again. Can you admit there's something between us that suggests—no, demands!—that we get to know one another better? I'm not going to rush you, Savvy, I just want to convince you to give us a chance."

Sky's voice was filled with entreaty. He was trying to be as gentle as he knew how to be. She could sense the intensity of his emotions in his heartfelt words. He wanted to be friends. Just like Hooker. No. She smiled secretly. *Not* like Hooker. She knew that, with every beat of her heart. And since she was being honest with herself, she wanted more than a platonic friendship too. If it were possible, she'd like to begin all over again and see if there was a chance for a lasting relationship.

She raised her thick lashes and gazed deeply into Sky's penetrating blue eyes. Her senses began to bubble like fine champagne as she dared to meet his challenge. Shyly she lifted her lips and kissed him. His soft growl of approval mingled with her delighted sigh. She could feel the sparks of their sweet meeting crackle around their attentive heads. There was something there all right, something well worth the effort of exploration. Although she could sense he was holding himself in firm control, she knew in another moment all barriers would be tossed aside.

She gently ended the kiss and smiled sensuously into his smoky eyes.

"My name is Savena Alexander. My friends call me Savvy. How do you do, Detective Skylar Brady?"

He continued to hold her close and brushed his warm lips across hers in a teasing, flirtatious kiss. "My friends call me Sky. And I'm doing fine, Savvy. I'm doing *better* than fine."

"Time enough for that later, lovebirds. My chicken Panne awaits!"

Savvy and Sky laughed half in embarrassment and half in good-natured humor. Hooker was a most insistent chef. With great aplomb, Sky seated Savvy, then sat down beside her to await the fanfare of the great gourmet. In moments Hooker reappeared pushing a heavily laden walnut serving cart. Chattering in a butchered French accent, he began his performance. With exaggerated expertise he opened the bottle of vintage wine and made a zany performance of getting Sky to taste and approve his choice. Then he filled three glasses and made a toast.

"To the three of us. May we all get our fondest wish." With nodding agreement, Sky and Savvy touched their tulip-shaped glasses to his and drank. Then Hooker began a quick recitation of the menu. With each announcement, he lifted a silver lid from a dish on the cart.

"The first course is spinach salad with Italian dressing. Both leaf and dressing have been prepared by culinary angels," he added, winking outrageously at Savvy, who winked right back. This time Sky just smiled indulgently at their playful performance.

"Next you will dine on my famous chicken Panne,

lightly breaded and sautéed, then topped with my secret cream and brandy sauce. *Magnifique!*" he exclaimed, kissing his fingertips. "This succulent cuisine will be enhanced by green beans almondine and feather-light croissants. And for dessert you will wallow in the creamy splendor of my *chocolat suprême.*"

Hooker murmured *bon appétit* as he made one final check that everything was as it should be. Then he lifted Savvy's hand to his lips, kissing her fingertips. "Enjoy your evening, my lovely. Sky will be your most attentive host."

"Aren't you going to dine with us?" Savvy's mouth suddenly grew dry. Hooker was leaving them alone. That much seemed evident. When he had left before, he obviously had gotten dressed to go out. His muscular body was now clad all in black—form-fitting trousers, silk shirt opened at the top to reveal dark luxuriantly thick curls.

His ebony hair gleamed in the candlelight and his dark eyes smoldered wickedly above his wide white smile. "Got a heavy date with a foxy lady," he said, pantomiming a torrid dance routine with a phantom partner.

"I didn't know you were interested in the study of wild life," Savvy teased. "A vixen, eh?"

Hooker gave her a playful kiss on the cheek and whispered enticingly into her ear. "I'm here to inform you, Ms. Alexander, that in high school I was nicknamed Hook-her . . . not Hook-*him!* You mustn't believe all you hear about male models. In my case, it's definitely not true."

She smiled up into his handsome face, thinking to

herself that he probably was a very able lover and she would be interested herself if it weren't for a particularly interesting detective she knew. Then her smile turned into a little smirk of disbelief and her eyes narrowed suspiciously. "And all this time I thought you got your name because you played around with basketballs!"

Sky immediately crumpled into laughter. He bent over from the waist and pointed accusingly at his friend, who had suddenly gone beet red. Savvy knew she had unearthed some lost treasures from the archives of their minds. Her remark hadn't been *that* funny! "Savvy has a talent for finding the truth, huh, Hooker, old man?"

By this time Hooker had regained his composure and chuckled self-deprecatingly. "I wouldn't touch that line with a ten-foot pole, buddy. And if you tell any tales about my youth, I'll be forced to reciprocate. You *do* understand, don't you? If she knew all about our hell-raisin' days, she'd call a cop!" His snide jab at Sky's profession sobered him considerably.

"Blood brothers, right?" He shook hands with Hooker in solemn silence. Then he slapped him on the back and gave him a shove toward the front door. "Have a good time. I won't wait up for you."

Not to be outdone, Hooker shot back a final volley. "If you do, it will be a first. I usually beat *you* home." With a wave and a thrown kiss for Savvy he was gone.

Sky turned back and eyed her with appreciation. "You certainly hit the nail on the head with your last remark."

"And I'll never know what skeleton-rattling closet I opened, will I?" She already knew the answer and she watched as Sky pulled the wheeled cart close to the table and reseated himself across from her.

"We go back a long way, Savvy," he answered, carefully dressing the salad. "I suppose he knows more about me than anyone else in the world."

"I'd like to know all about you, Sky." He met her sincere gaze with a surprised expression. It seemed as if he was having a little trouble believing her.

"Would you?"

She nodded eagerly and leaned forward. "Tell me *everything*," she whispered, her snapping eyes sparking golden in the candlelight.

Four

Sky leaned back in his chair and thoughtfully sipped at his wine. His narrowed eyes glinted over the rim of the glass as he gazed at her animated, alert features. Wary of her sincerity he made an observation, rather than begin the story of his life. "You just want to get me to talk so you won't have to."

She blinked with studied innocence. "That's not true, Sky. I *do* want to know about your life." Lifting her glass, she drank the last of her wine, then searched Sky's face as if she were making a decision about something. When she spoke again, she met his measuring gaze with direct, clear eyes. "I'll admit," she confessed softly, "that your words are *partly* true, but only partly. It seems to me, if we're to have a friendship, we *both* have to show some trust and commitment."

Sky laughed easily at her rebuttal. "You should have been a lawyer, Savvy. You're a pro at clouding the issue to your own advantage."

"But I'm making sense, right?"

"Right."

"Good! You go first."

He laughed again and shook his head. "See?" But Savvy refused to say another word; instead, she sat quietly waiting. And Sky knew he had lost this round. "I was born and raised on a small ranch about fifty miles from here, west of Bartlesville. My great-grandfather won the property in a poker game. Years later his son became the local sheriff. Pappy was quite a man. He taught me a lot and put up with a lot. As Hooker indicated, even as a child I was a handful."

"We have that in common," Savvy interjected, chuckling wickedly. "I'd like to hear some of his stories about you."

"Pappy died when I was twelve," he answered softly. "I still miss him, especially when I need someone to talk to."

Savvy had the feeling that his loss was much greater than he inferred. "Are your folks still living?"

Sorrow shadowed his usually bright features. It was a moment before he spoke again. "My mother died six months before my grandfather. It was very sudden. We had virtually no warning. I always thought her passing was the cause of Pappy's death. He just lost his fire when she left us." He stared into the flickering candle flame in the center of their small table, lost in thought. Savvy waited silently until he could pull himself back to the present and speak again. "It took me a long time to get over their deaths." Shaking his head slightly, he refilled both their glasses from the wine bottle.

"You still had your dad, didn't you?"

"Yeah, but he was lost too. We made quite a maudlin pair. Just when I thought we were coming out of it, he died in his sleep. It was five years to the day that Mom passed away. It took me months to realize that Dad probably felt just like Pappy had, only he kept going for me."

Savvy had tears in her eyes. Her heart was breaking for the sad youth who had lost everyone he loved in such a short time. Silently she counted her blessing of healthy, loving parents who had seen her through many a teenage crisis and still cared deeply about her welfare. She reached across the table and placed her warm hand over his larger, stronger one. "You must have only been about seventeen years old," she said. "Who took care of you then?"

"My dad had written his will so that Hooker's parents were appointed my guardians until I was eighteen. I've always believed he knew I'd just need a little time before I'd take off. He was right of course. When I graduated from high school I joined the army. Hooker went with me. After our hitch we came back to Tulsa, where I went to the Police Academy. And then I met you." He smiled broadly. "That's about it."

But Savvy had a dozen questions she wanted answered. "Who took care of your ranch while you were gone? Who takes care of it now?"

"Mr. and Mrs. Jablonski, to both questions," he replied. "I'd like you to see my place. I think you'll like it." He stopped suddenly. It seemed as if he were catching himself from saying more. "That is, if you ever *do* come home with me for a weekend."

His words made Savvy feel very uncomfortable. First he assumed too much. Now he was pulling back. Why? she wondered. Perhaps he was having second thoughts about a friendship with her. She tried to throw off her uneasy feeling by asking an unrelated question. "Do you plant crops on your land? Or is it a cattle ranch?"

Sky seemed relieved at the change of subject. "Until about fifty years ago, the Rocking B. was a working farm and cattle ranch. Then things changed. We're very limited now. We grow just enough hay for a small herd and some quarter horses."

"How come?"

"The oil wells got in the way."

She sat up to attention, her eyes wide with astonishment. "You are rich!"

In answer, Sky shrugged to downplay her surprise. "Comfortable, at least," he agreed, serving the next course of their meal. The succulent food put an end to their conversation while they enjoyed it. As they were finishing dessert, Savvy was bursting to ask another question.

"If you're so rich, why in the world do you stay on the police force?" she wondered aloud.

"It's in my blood, I guess. Fourth generation. My father was a judge and my great-grandfather was the local J.P. Married 'em, buried 'em, and made the laws in between." He chuckled, thinking how many times he had said those words.

"Do you want to do police work the rest of your life?" Savvy did not realize that her question was a pointed one. She was only thinking that she would be frightened for him if she were his wife. Caught by this unexpected thought, it was a moment before she saw the change on Sky's face. He was looking at her with a grim, hard expression. "Wait!" she begged hurriedly. "The question wasn't meant to be condescending. I just think your work is terribly dangerous. Don't be angry."

His steely gaze lost some of its chill with his short reply. "I'm formulating some plans for the future."

When no more information was forthcoming, Savvy prodded. "Well?"

"I haven't finished my research yet. I'll be glad to share it with you when I've completed my study," he answered. His steady voice held the same tone as a stranger giving an oral report. Then he added, "If you're still around."

His cryptic reply puzzled Savvy. He was backing off again. Was this trust and commitment to a new friendship? she asked herself. With an outward calm she rose from the table and walked to the window to stare at the star-studded night sky. She wasn't used to being treated like a discarded or unwanted guest and her pride took over. Her voice was low and cool when she spoke. "Look, why don't we just cancel this discussion? You seem to understand what you're saying, but I certainly don't. You give a little trust by sharing. Then you take it all away with a few well-chosen words." Her voice broke a little, but she continued. "You claim you've been trying to see me for a month, but just now you wonder if I'll ever see your home or be interested in your plans for the future. What is this?" She turned to face him. "I won't be treated like a fool. You don't really care." Feeling her composure crack she quickly turned away again. "I honestly don't think you even like me." She swallowed hard and willed herself not to lean against him when he came to stand behind her.

"Maybe I care so much, I find it's almost impossible to give you my complete trust," he whispered in a bewildered voice.

"What's that supposed to mean?" she shot back almost before he was finished speaking.

"It would take too long to explain right now."

Another cryptic statement, she thought, seething. Well, he wasn't going to get by with it, she vowed. She turned to him and muttered, "Try me."

He appeared unruffled by her dare. "Another time, Savvy. Right now it's your turn to tell me a little about your childhood."

His composure destroyed hers. "Why bother?" she asked, using the same cool tone he had used earlier. "We probably won't be seeing one another again anyway."

Before Savvy had a chance to twist her head away, Sky kissed her, hard. His overpowering mastery stole her strength and began to replace her anger with passion. When the kiss ended, he held her close to his firm, warm body and spoke against her flaxen hair. "We won't talk about the future now. We'll just take it one step at a time. Now let's have your bio."

Although she had to hold on to him to keep from

collapsing in his arms, she had one last bit of fight left in her. "I won't be interrogated, Detective Brady."

He pulled away from her just far enough to gaze down into her flashing green eyes and smile sweetly. "Please?" When he smiled like a cherished leprechaun, she had no more defense. He held her chair for her and she took a fortifying drink from her glass before she began her recitation.

"I was born in Springfield, Missouri. When I was ten we moved to a small farm outside of town. My folks still live there. We raise quarter horses just as you do. I'm an only child. Are you?"

He nodded.

"Something else we have in common," she said. "I decided to settle in Tulsa after I graduated from the university here. End of story."

"How long have you been bothered by claustrophobia?"

She hadn't expected the question. At least not so soon. Remembering again the circumstances of their first meeting, she lowered her lashes in embarrassment. It was her turn to back off, but by gosh, she decided, she was going to go on the offensive. She lifted her eyes to meet his steady, patient gaze. "So now we get to the real reason for this question-and-answer session." She didn't want to be reminded about the elevator and she stood again to walk away.

But Sky caught her within his strong embrace and kissed her again. She moaned softly when the heat of his lips lit fiery rockets in the pit of her stomach. It seemed so unfair that he could use his warm, supple mouth as a weapon against her determination not to discuss the matter. Although his heart was beating in tandem with her runaway pulse, he stayed in control and ended the kiss. He lifted his lips only a fraction of an inch. She could feel his words on her own mouth. "How long?"

She pondered his insistent question, then finally gave in and told him. Although Sky seemed to be listening to her explanation, he was barely hearing her because he was thinking about her body and how good it felt held close to his. She could feel the change in his touch and was not surprised when, after her explanation, he began to shower her throat and ear lobe with gentle, attentive kisses.

"I'm sorry you get so frightened," he crooned softly into her ear, setting her on fire when he traced the outline with his moist pointed tongue. "I'm glad I was there for you when you needed me." Silently he heard other words within his heart. Oh, Lord! Now the situation was turned around. He needed her . . . so much. Wanting her, he moved closer and trailed his fingertips across her firm, proud breast. Immediately Savvy froze in his arms.

"You'd better take me home, Sky."

He removed his hand and instead tried to massage the stiffness from her spine. "You're remembering again."

"And aren't you?" she countered, beginning to feel angry again.

Sky continued to hold and mold her to his length. "I remember that I felt incredibly happy and absolutely fascinated and wildly excited when I was holding you in my arms in that dark elevator. All you remember is your terror."

"And *foolishness*!"

Her last remark made him give up in disgust. "Oh, hell! Let's go." Without another word he blew out the candle and led the way out the front door, handing her her purse from the side table in the entry as they left.

Bewildered, Savvy followed. Why was she so upset? She had gotten exactly what she wanted, hadn't she? He had gotten carried away with memories of their first meeting, just as she had known he would. Why had she ever hoped it might be different? No man forgets when a woman throws herself at him. It was like catnip . . . he would never be satisfied until he had it all!

Sky helped Savvy into his car; his touch was not as gentle as before. As he walked around to the driver's side he castigated himself for his lack of reserve and control. He had known how mixed up she was about their mutually rewarding time during her entrapment in the elevator. Why had he hoped she would change her thinking and realize he cared for *her*? He should have his head examined, he decided angrily. Above all he needed to be reminded that he couldn't always have what he wanted. Well, he didn't have to be hit by a truck, he told himself. He would take her home and say good-bye. And that would be the end of it. His smoldering passion laughed right in his face. Who was he trying to kid?

The ride back to Savvy's apartment was silent and rapid. She refused to ask him to slow down and he didn't seem inclined to honor her request if she had asked. When he pulled into the parking place next to her van, she began to open the door to get out.

"I'll say good night here, Sky."

But Sky growled that he would see her to the door. With his barked command, he threw his door wide and banged it against the side of the van. "Dammit!" he exploded, getting out and stalking around to her side.

She jumped out and stood toe to toe with his tense body. "Don't you take your mean temper out on Violet," she yelled. "She was here first."

Her lusty comment broke the tension and Sky laughed gruffly. "Sorry, Violet." He sighed, taking Savvy's hand and leading her to the steps of her apartment. He could tell that she didn't want him to see her to her door, but he was just as determined to have his way. He glanced up at her living-room sliding door and noticed that the light was on by the couch. "Do you have a timer on your light?" he asked conversationally, but his heart had begun to pound with foreboding. He'd put Jocko out of commission for a long time if the little bastard had sent members of his gang to Savvy's home to wreck the place. When she answered that she didn't have one, he stood her against the wall at the foot of her stairs and asked for her key. When she found it in her purse and handed it to him, he gave her a crisp order to stay where she was, then silently climbed the steps and withdrew his service revolver from the holster at the back of his trousers.

The click of the lock seemed to reverberate along his spine. Stealthily he pushed the door open and glanced through the crack to make sure no one was hiding behind. With his revolver held ready against any movement, Sky went through the entire apartment, opening closet doors, searching under her bed and in back of furniture. Adrenaline was pumping through his system, readying his body for anything. Balancing himself on the balls of his feet like a boxer preparing for the fight of his life, Sky threw open the last closed door, and instead of finding a second bedroom he could see that the area was Savvy's office and storage space. On shelves at the far end of the room were several of her samples and prototypes for upcoming special events and business meetings. A teddy bear stared back at him from atop a wicker basket filled with silk flowers that was attached to a bright pink helium-filled balloon, straining at its tether. The greeting on the balloon read, It's a Girl! On another shelf a sparkling gold dollar sign caught his eye. It, too, was nestled in a base of silk flowers with streamers rising to their bobbing spheres. He assumed this was an idea for a sales-award banquet or some similar function. Before he could assess the remainder of her creative centerpieces, Savvy called from the doorway of her apartment.

"Sky? Sky, is everything all right?" Her voice quavered a little because she had expected him back sooner and was alarmed. Had he surprised someone trying to rob her apartment? she wondered worriedly. "Sky? *Answer me.*"

Flicking off the light, Sky closed the office door behind him and returned to the living room. "Everything seems to be in order," he said. Why, Savvy wondered, did he have that silly grin on his face? She watched as he returned his revolver to his holster and walked over to the floor lamp. "Now let's see if we can figure this fixture's tricks," he added in a most happy and reasonable voice. She didn't know that he had done a very thorough job of searching her home and had found absolutely no evidence of a roommate—female or male! As he fiddled with the light switch on the lamp it began to go off and on like a neon advertisement. "Ah, I think I've discovered the problem. The socket somehow worked itself loose and went on all by itself." In a minute he had tightened the loose piece and stood proudly turning the switch on and off. And all the while he was smiling. "That should take care of it, Savvy."

"Why are you grinning like the cat that swallowed the canary?" she asked. She hated not being in on a joke.

Sky didn't answer her, but asked a question instead. "I take it that you live here alone?"

Savvy's eyes narrowed suspiciously. "What makes you ask that?"

"Oh, when I was here earlier, waiting for you to change clothes, I noticed you had two place mats on your table."

She laughed at his obvious smokescreen. The man wanted to know if he had any competition, especially some that was already on the premises. He already knew she lived alone, she decided, thinking about his search. Besides, she had never been able to act cute or coy. "My mother sent them to me. It's her way of telling me she thinks I should have a friend. Nothing like a matchmaking mother. She might as well have sent me a telegram."

The lamp went off again, but this time it was Sky's hand that was responsible. The only light left on was the one in the kitchen, which illuminated the living room with a soft glow. She watched as he walked toward her and gathered her into his warm embrace. It felt wonderful when he held her. She felt safe and protected somehow. "I'm glad you live alone, Savvy," he whispered tenderly.

She could barely find breath enough to ask why.

Leaning close, he sidestepped the whole truth— that he was becoming more and more attracted to her—and answered on a murmured sigh. "Because I'm going to kiss you good night and I don't want to be interrupted, honey."

Five

Savvy was tying her running shoes when the phone rang. It was six A.M. Who could that be? she wondered. Maybe Teri was going to cancel out.

"Hello?"

"Morning, Savvy. Did I wake you?" It was Sky, and he sounded as if he'd been up for hours.

She squirmed like a happy puppy and smiled while she balanced on one foot to tie the laces of her other shoe. "Good morning, Sky," she answered brightly. "You didn't wake me. In fact, you just caught me before I left for my run. I always try to get an early start, especially with this heat wave. What's up?"

He was silent for a moment, thinking about her strong, shapely body running like the wind. "I'll bet you look great in running shorts," he said with a little catch in his voice.

Savvy closed her eyes and visualized again her first impression of his great body dropping down out of the sky. What a sculptured physique! Shaking herself from her reverie, she stood straight and brought the conversation back to the present. "Is there some reason for your call . . . besides your hope that you'd wake me?" she teased softly.

"Yeah, kid. I've got the day off and hoped we could spend some time together. Can we?" Savvy could tell by the tone of his voice that he was grinning confidently. And again she thought about his strength and wished she had the time for a game of racquetball with him. If she was really on her toes, she could beat him . . . maybe.

"I've got a mountain of work to do today, Sky. Remember, there's no one to replace me if I take time off. I'm sorry." She explained that as soon as she finished her run she had to go to Mr. Goldblum's to pick up supplies for an upcoming party.

"We can still meet for lunch," he countered. "You have to eat, you know. Look, I was just leaving for the gym. Why don't we meet in his lobby and I'll help you haul the supplies? What time will you be there?"

She hesitated while her disciplined self held a losing battle with her playful side. "I should get there about eight-thirty," she answered. "It won't take more than an hour to gather the order so why don't we plan on having brunch instead? I really do have lots of work to do this afternoon," she added.

THE LIGHT SIDE • 81

"Sounds great to me, honey," he replied. "Will you be wearing your clown outfit or can I look for the best-looking gal in Tulsa?"

"Either way you won't find me," she bantered. "I'll be wearing street clothes today. No birthdays to celebrate."

"I'd find you, Savvy," he shot back, causing a heat wave of emotion to flow over her skin when she heard the conviction in his words. "Are you warmed up yet?"

"*What?*"

"Have you warmed up for your run?" he elaborated patiently. "You don't want to pull a muscle."

"Yes, I'm warmed up . . . and I'm leaving now. I'll see you soon." Before she could hang up the receiver she heard an echo of a sensuous, deep chuckle, and suddenly she knew she had gotten his veiled message correct the first time! She shrugged as she started out the door, knowing it would be a waste of energy to huff and puff about it when no one was here to see her. Instead she grinned from ear to ear, secretly enjoying his outrageous question. "That silver-tongued Irish devil," she exclaimed, laughing out loud as she ran down the steps to meet Teri.

When she got to the corner, Teri was running in place and reading the morning newspaper at the same time. As Savvy slowed to run beside her, her friend gave her a big hug and squealed happily. "You've made the front page, Savena Alexander. You're a bloomin' hero—ine!" Then she showed her the story about the capture of Jocko. The piece included a large photograph of Savvy sitting atop the boy while Papa Delgadio stood guard.

"I didn't see any reporter," she exclaimed, grabbing the paper and devouring the story. "My parents are going to have a fit if they find out," she added with a frown. "Oh, why did they have to do this?"

Teri laughed and hugged her again. "It isn't every day that a clown captures a purse snatcher, my girl. This is news. Besides, think of all the free publicity. It mentions your business right in the first paragraph."

Half-perturbed and half-excited at the prospect of more business, Savvy stuck the folded paper in the back of her elastic waistband and gave her friend a gently shove toward the parkway. "Come on, Pegasus. After this news I need a run more than ever," she exhorted while wondering what Sky would think of the article.

As they always did each morning, Savvy and Teri shared the events of the day before. Savvy did the bulk of the talking this morning. Teri wanted to know *everything*! And since she was Savvy's best friend, she learned *almost* everything too. But both were past their teen years when best friends told all. It was an unspoken agreement between them . . . and knowing one another so well it was fairly easy to fill in the gaps anyway. But when Savvy told her about Sky Brady, Teri crowed with delight.

"Oh, Savvy. Maybe he's the one. It's about time you found a man for yourself."

"I might say the same thing to you," she teased back. "We're the happy workaholics."

"Yeah, but it's more exciting when we have some diversion. All work and no play, you know!" Her wide eyes danced gleefully when she gave Savvy a little smack on the seat. "Come on, career girl. I'll race you on the home stretch."

After Savvy had showered and shampooed her hair, she dressed quickly in comfortable chino culottes and a lavender knit top. Stepping into her high-heeled sandals, she grabbed her purse and skipped down the steps to her van. Remembering last night's mishap with Sky's car door, she examined the side and saw a new little dent. Patting Violet's latest injury, she wondered what damage Sky had done to his own car. Served him right, she decided, climbing in and starting the engine. That fiery temper had probably gotten him into a lot of trouble, she thought, smiling. But as she backed from her parking spot her smile was replaced with a little frown. "I could be the one with a whole lot of trouble," she muttered, reliving his ardent kiss at her door. She tooted her horn at Papa Delgadio, who was busily sweeping his sidewalk as she passed. She was smiling again, thinking happily about her date with Sky. "But a little diversion won't hurt," she decided aloud.

Sky was waiting outside the building when she pulled to the curb. His smile and intense smoky eyes made Savvy feel the warmth of his visual touch. He had the clean-cut look of an athlete with his muscular body clad in form-fitting jeans and a crisp blue shirt—the color of the sky, she thought playfully—with the short sleeves rolled twice to reveal his bulging biceps. His thumbs were hooked into his front pants pockets and he was leaning against the brick wall, in the shade, one booted foot crossed over the other. He waved when he saw her and straightened up to walk to her side of the van. Pulling the door open he slipped his hands around her waist and gently lifted her to the ground. She suspected it was no accident that he slid her slowly along his length as he helped her down. She thought again of how lovely it felt to be held in his arms, and her eyes must have revealed her inner feelings because Sky's smile widened into a warm, knowing grin.

"Hi, pretty lady. How was your run?"

"Great, but I needed it more this morning than I usually do."

Sky raised an inquiring eyebrow. Savvy knew he was thinking it was because of his call. She couldn't hold back a little laugh. "Have you seen the paper today?"

When he said that he hadn't, she handed him the front page and he read it as they walked back to the entrance of Mr. Goldblum's building. "It's a good picture of you, Savvy," he said, folding the paper and handing it back to her. His face was serious as he stood beside her, lost in thought. He didn't like the idea of this story being plastered all over the newspaper. It would be just the sort of thing to make Jocko madder than hell, he thought. Little hoods like him could take almost anything except a bruise to the ego. Being captured by a female clown wouldn't sit well with him, Sky knew. And he began to worry again about Savvy's safety.

Savvy, of course, could not decipher his worried expression. Could he be upset because he wasn't mentioned in the story? she wondered. But then she put the thought out of her mind, knowing Sky wasn't like that at all. "Don't you like the story, Sky?" she asked in a small voice.

He brought his eyes back to her worried face and his lighted up dramatically. "It's a great story, Savvy. And it should get a whole lot of inquiries about your business too." He took her hand and began to walk through the lobby.

"That's what Teri said."

He stopped in his tracks. "Who's Terry?" he asked suspiciously.

Savvy read that thought loud and clear. "Teri is my best friend. T-e-r-i. We run together."

His face shone with a relieved smile. "I'm glad you run with someone. I wouldn't want you to run alone." He looked thoughtful. "Even so, I think I'll give you a police whistle just in case."

"Just in case of what?"

"Like I said, you're a very pretty lady, honey."

Because they had been deep in conversation Savvy wasn't aware that he had pushed the button for the elevator, so she was surprised when it opened right in front of her. "Wait a minute, Sky. I don't use these things, remember?" She began to back away from the terrifying, ornate box. "I use the stairs."

Sky slipped his arm around her slim waist and gently but firmly led her toward the door. "Come on, Savvy. Give it a try. You won't be alone. Let's see if you can fight those dark devils if I'm here to help you. Okay?"

"This is against my better judgment," she said as she shakily entered the elevator. When he hit the button for the sixth floor and they began to rise inside the shaft, Savvy nervously grabbed him around his middle and held on for dear life.

Sky held her tight and began a soothing, continuous banter of words against her ear. "I'm here, honey. Just listen to my voice. Don't pay attention to anything else. Just focus on my words and you'll be just fine. Trust me."

She was totally amazed when, in a few moments, the doors slid apart and she was led, wide-eyed and surprised, out the sixth-floor entry and into Mr. Goldblum's office. "I did it," she whispered. "I didn't think I ever could."

"I'll send you my bill in the morning," Sky teased, but his eyes showed how proud he was of her.

Mr. Goldblum's face lit up at her entrance. "Ah, little dove. I am so happy to see you again." He nodded to Sky. "I see now that you are so famous you have a bodyguard." He chuckled. "I suppose that means I won't be able to get my hello kiss."

"I really shouldn't kiss you, my friend," she scolded playfully. "After all, you acted as Sky's informant. How will I ever be able to trust you again?" she asked, diluting her little speech with her usual kiss to his wrinkled cheek.

"I love intrigue, my dove," he admitted while his china blue eyes twinkled in delight. "Now, what can I get for you?"

It was almost forty-five minutes before Savvy's order was filled. Sky watched in amazement as the pile of boxes and materials grew into a small mountain, but he said nothing. After she signed for the order and promised payment at the end of the week, he began to stack the things onto a dolly and told them both he would be right back. In a minute he stuck his head around the door and told Savvy he was all set.

"Good. I'll meet you downstairs then," Savvy replied, giving Mr. Goldblum another peck on his cheek before she followed Sky.

But Sky had other ideas. "Whoa, gal! Aren't you coming with me?" He was holding her arm and had locked his challenging gaze with her fearful eyes. "You can do it. I know it, honey," he cajoled.

"I think once is all my nervous system can take for the day," she pleaded, trying to slip out of his firm grip.

"Come on, Savvy. Give it a try." He led her gently to the propped-open doors. "I'll hold you," he coaxed softly. "You'll make it."

At first she seemed fine, but then the elevator gave a disquieting buck and she lost all control. "I can't," she screamed hysterically. "Sky, let me out."

She tore away from him and began to beat against the buttons, trying desperately to escape. Instantly Sky pulled her into a captive embrace and kissed her. He held her breathlessly tight, pushing all the air from her lungs while he tried to deepen his kiss against her quivering lips. Savvy became almost faint from hyperventilation, and her screams subsided to whimpers of distress as he held her and kissed her to distraction. When the elevator doors slid open on the ground floor, Savvy was participating fully in Sky's diversionary tactic, moving her body against his hips and holding his head with her frantic, searching hands. Mentally, she was nowhere but in Sky's arms. Fear had been driven from her mind. She could feel

Sky's heart hammering in his chest. In a daze she parted her lips. His moist, warm tongue explored her and the kiss went on . . . and on . . . and on. Now that the elevator had stopped Savvy never wanted the kiss to end.

"You gonna stay in there all day, buddy?" A man's gruff challenging words foggily entered the pair's consciousness.

Slowly Sky broke the kiss, adding several smaller kisses to Savvy's pouting love-swollen mouth. As he gazed down into Savvy's dazed features, he said quietly to the man, "Naw, we're gonna go home and cool off."

"Fat chance of that!" the man exploded, chuckling wickedly.

Red-faced and fuming, Savvy grabbed several items and marched with her head erect out the door to her van. Throwing the boxes in the back, she railed at Sky, who had followed close behind. "Sky, you've got to stop trying to run my life. I'm not going swimming with you. I have a million things to do today."

Undaunted, Sky straightened the scattered boxes and continued his calm, reasonable persuasion. "We'll need a swim after we get all these things up to your apartment. We can pick up your suit and go to my place. I'd planned on our brunch there anyway. Hooker promised to make us shrimp salad before he left this morning for an assignment," he tempted. "He'll be madder than a hornet if we don't eat it. You don't want me to get fat by eating all of it myself, do you?"

Thinking that Sky didn't have an extra ounce of flesh on his beautiful frame, Savvy relented with a laugh. "This is one for you," she conceded, "but I can't stay long."

"I wouldn't think of keeping you from your business," he replied in a serious voice, but his dancing eyes told her quite plainly that he was going to have a hell of a good time trying!

"Your ego is showing, Detective Brady. It's swelling up like a big fat balloon filled with hot air."

"But you've got me wrapped around your little finger, Ms. Alexander," he countered, playfully twisting the small diamond ring around her little finger.

She grabbed her hand away and climbed into her van. "Fat chance of that, buster!" Joining in his playful mood, she asked with a giggle, "Suppose I told you I don't have a swimming suit . . . and that I don't skinny-dip in broad daylight?"

"Do you at night?" he shot back, his dark eyes smoldering.

"Leading question, officer," she said, then drove off, laughing again when she glanced into the rearview mirror and saw him run to his car to follow her.

Savvy was indeed ready for a cooling swim after she and Sky had hauled everything up the stairway to her apartment. She stuffed her swimming suit into a carryall along with a beach towel and sun screen, then announced that she was all set. In a short time they were racing up another stairway, this time to the second floor of Sky's mansion.

"How many bedrooms do you have up here?" she asked, walking along the long hallway.

"Eight in all," he answered, opening the door to a

room. "You use this one. It's mine. I'll change across the hall."

She really didn't want to use his room. It seemed so personal. But she couldn't make an issue of it either. Besides, she'd like to see where he slept! Closing the door behind her she took in the large room in one quick glance, then began to explore seriously. Overall it was definitely a man's room. Warm browns and navy blues enhanced heavy walnut furniture and gold accents. She thought the huge bed covered with a tailored navy spread was even larger than her king-sized one at home. Impossible! she decided, walking over to the dresser, which displayed family photographs. She touched the gilt frame of one large picture and saw it was a family group—Sky's father and mother and him. He looked about eleven years old, so it must have been taken shortly before his mother died. Savvy looked more closely. The woman in the picture didn't appear to be ill at all. It must have been a terrible shock, she thought, remembering Sky's words about having no warning. Next to the picture was another one in sepia tones. A dapper man stared at her, a bold smile curving his handlebar mustache. His eyes held the same devilish gleam as Sky's. She decided this had to be a photograph of Pappy, Sky's grandfather. The picture was a full-length pose and she could readily see that Sky had inherited his strong body from his mother's side of the family. "I'll bet he drove the ladies wild," she whispered, giggling softly.

Knowing she had spent more time than she should have, she hurried into the adjoining bathroom to change clothes. She smiled at her reflection in the mirror when she put on her skimpy bikini. It had a turquoise bottom and a strip of the same fabric for a narrow bandeau top that was covered with three rainbow ruffles—pink, turquoise, and purple. Assessing her figure with a critical eye, she smiled again, wondering if she just might be able to drive a particular man wild. She picked up her towel and lotion before she strolled out into the hallway, but then she skidded to a stop. Sky was leaning indolently against the door frame across the way. His eyes narrowed in his own assessment of her trim body.

"*Very nice*, honey," he murmured as his smoldering gaze trailed along her curves.

Savvy stood fused to the floor, refusing to blush and be further disturbed by his almost nude body skimpily clad in wicked black racing briefs. She gulped once and decided to play the game. "I'll return the compliment, *honey*!"

He moved to her side and brushed a strand of champagne-colored hair behind her ear. "Don't you like to be called 'honey'?"

"Don't say it if you don't mean it," she answered, unconsciously echoing his former date's words, intensely aware of the heat of his body radiating into hers.

"Oh, I mean it, honey. For the first time in my life . . . *I mean it*!" He took her hand and led her down the stairs to the back of the house and outside.

The pool shone like a glittering jewel in the late morning sunlight. Tossing their towels on a chaise longue they dove cleanly into the water and began to swim laps. Both were excellent swimmers and soon they were synchronized in their strokes, happily gliding up and down the length of the pool. Finally exhausted, Savvy pulled herself up on the edge and lay down in the warm sunshine. Moments later Sky followed her. He rolled a double lounge out of the shade and invited her to join him. Feeling relaxed and sleepy, Savvy declined.

"I don't want to move, Sky," she answered in a breathy voice. Before she could draw another deep breath, he picked her up and carried her to the lounge, depositing her gently on the smooth, soft fabric. "Nothing like having a strong man around the house," she said dreamily, rolling over on her stomach and snuggling against the mattress.

"You're going to burn," Sky murmured, and Savvy's eyes popped open in alarm. Were his words a warning against the sun or a promise of his charms? she wondered, feeling the adrenaline churn through her veins in readiness for anything. "I'd better put lotion on you before you do." He smiled knowingly when he heard Savvy's expulsion of air at his added words.

"Mmmm, that feels wonderful," she purred, squirming a little under his tender touch. "I don't know how a man as strong as you can have such gentle hands."

He continued to smooth the lotion over her shoulders, arms, and back and worked his way along her long, trim legs. "You're strong, Savvy, but you're still a woman. I wouldn't want to hurt you, honey."

Again Savvy read an additional meaning into his words, not aware that Sky was also silently warning himself about being hurt by her. He didn't know if he could take another disappointment from life. "Turn over, woman. You're getting pink already," he said, rolling her easily onto her back. She lay with her eyes closed against the noonday sun, but she could feel his lingering gaze wander over her relaxed body. "You're one beautiful lady," he said, desire evident in his hoarse voice.

Savvy smiled serenely and replied in like manner. "And you're one beautiful man."

"I love to look at you," he added, beginning to apply more lotion to her skin. "I know you work out just as I do, but I'd be the first to admit you've gotten great results from time well spent." His touch changed subtly and Savvy was aware that his breathing had become rough and deeper. She knew she had to do something before she got in over her head with him.

Lazily she sat up and took the bottle from his hand. "Your turn, Sky. We don't want you to get heat stroke," she teased softly, beginning to rub his back and arms.

"I don't even feel the heat of the sun," he argued quietly. "That's not what I'm feeling at all!"

She acted as if she didn't hear him and ordered him to lie down on his stomach while she applied her sun screen to his skin. Talk about peak experiences! She could trace all the different muscle groups across his back. His legs, she decided, were like pillars of granite, and his shoulders looked as if they had been sculpted in bronze. "You have a nice tan," she crooned. Just as she was gaining some control over her emotions, he rolled over onto his back and she was almost completely lost with just one glance at his broad, well-defined chest. The curls made a thick mat of gold that narrowed and disappeared beneath his skin-tight briefs. Tentatively she began to smooth on the lotion, but her hands were trembling and she had begun to breathe erratically.

Sky caught her slender fingers in a strong hand, simultaneously lifting his body over hers and taking her into his arms. "Who are we trying to kid, Savvy? All I've been thinking about since I left you last night was needing to kiss you again." He didn't wait for her agreement or refusal. Lowering his head he covered her mouth with his, quickly deepening their kiss when he felt her complete surrender. She made a deep mewing sound and wrapped her arms around him, urging him closer to her slippery body. He pulled away gently and smiled down into her smoldering emerald eyes. "The kiss on the elevator doesn't count. That was fear. But now you know exactly what you're doing."

Savvy nodded dreamily and agreed. "I'm not afraid now."

He groaned in satisfaction and kissed her again, thrusting his tongue between her straight white teeth, wanting to drink all her sweetness into his aroused, parched body. His hands began a slow exploration of her curved body, and soon Savvy brought him fully alive with her tender search across his chest and tense back. When Sky's lips followed the pathway of his touch, she was thrown directly into the center of passion. He kissed the rounded swells of her breasts and blazed a hot trail down her abdomen to her exposed navel. When he moved to kiss her hip bone, she shuddered against him. He slid his hand beneath her to knead and massage the softness of her bottom, slipping his fingers inside her suit. She caressed his throat, exciting his throbbing pulse point there. Sighing throatily, he rolled against her, making her totally aware of his arousal as his hand moved between her legs and began to delve into her secret heat. "I want to make love with you, Savvy," he whispered against her breasts. Nudging her top down, he pulled a hard bud into his mouth and sucked eagerly. His actions were electric. So intense was Savvy's reaction that she lifted herself against him and encouraged him with her movement to take his fill. He answered her silent call by removing her bandeau and feasting on both firm breasts. Moving his hand back to the warmth between her legs, he raised his head and their gazes locked with passion. "I think you want to make love with me too," he said, then sighed harshly. "God, honey, please don't say no. *Not now.*" She could hear the pain of his need in his hoarse voice.

Kissing him on the shoulder and moving her lips to his hard flat nipple, she gave him her answer. "I'm not saying no, Sky. I want to make love *with you.*"

Without another word Sky gathered her into his arms and walked into the house. All the while he kissed her hair and curled her against his body, smiling when she tightened her hold around his neck and buried her face against his throat, nibbling teasingly. Effortlessly he carried her up the stairs to his bedroom. Before he placed her on the bed he crooned against her ear, keeping her face hidden at his shoulder.

"Are you protected, Savvy?"

A quick shake of her head gave him his answer and somehow he was suddenly relieved. "I'll take care of you, honey. Don't worry about a thing." He balanced her in his arms and threw back the spread, then set her down on the firm mattress. Smiling into her smoky green eyes, he threw her a kiss then walked to the windows and closed the drapes. The room became veiled in cool shadows, but Savvy could still see clearly as he moved to his dresser, withdrew a packet from the drawer, then slowly removed his swimming trunks before he turned back to her. She had never seen such a fantastic male body. He walked with grace and control. He would be a very aggressive, competent lover, she decided with the last part of her brain that was not yet consumed with her desire for him.

He stood at the bedside, unselfconscious about his arousal. "You're so very beautiful, Savvy. I want you. See how much I want to make love with you?"

In answer she lifted her weightless hand to stroke his thigh, running her fingers from his knee to his hip. She could feel the effect of her touch by his shudder of passion. He sank to his knees and removed her suit, then began to worship her body in a way Savvy had never experienced before. "I want to taste you. I want to touch you everywhere. I want to know you as well as I know myself," he murmured, gathering her into his arms and kissing her sensuously. "I want you more than I've ever wanted anything in my life."

When she could stand no more of this one-sided foreplay, she coaxed him to her side and moved over him. "My turn now," she pleaded. "You can't have all the fun."

He collapsed on the pillow beside her and smiled happily, crooning with that same keening sound she remembered from their first encounter when she had moved across his hips. She adored giving him pleasure, she decided with a little grin, and bent to her task with loving hands and lips. Soon he was having a truly difficult time lying still beneath her exploring touch. With easy grace he pushed her onto her back and rolled against her. "That's enough for now, little lady," he whispered brokenly. "I want you eager and ready for me *now*. You've done your job too damn well!" Then he kissed her and caressed her moist center as he put actions to words. She couldn't have said afterward all that he had done to her body. She only knew she went slowly out of her mind with her need for his complete possession.

Writhing against his probing touch, murmuring between hot kisses, she tried to show him that she was more eager than she had ever hoped to be. "I want you, Sky," she cried. "Please, don't make me wait any longer. I can't stand it."

Her impassioned words finally broke Sky's control. He moved over Savvy and filled her with his fire, driving her into complete oblivion. She felt light-headed and almost faint as he took her to the heights, but her strong body surged with his every thrust. She rose to meet him each time, reveling with him in total abandonment to their desire. When they came to the edge of passion, Savvy cried out his name and convulsed beneath his churning hips. And when he shuddered in total release she knew she would never be the same again. Who could ever wish to top the performance of Superman? she mused, feeling herself pulled against his relaxed body before she drifted into a dreamless sleep.

It was late in the afternoon when Savvy was awakened by warm lips nestling against her breasts. She groaned, still half asleep, as she moved to give the explorer greater access to her flesh. "I must have fallen asleep," she murmured drowsily. "Sorry."

"I slept too, honey. Better than I have in a month."

"Now *you're* remembering," she warned, pushing his head away so she could sit up. But she felt so happy that she couldn't work up a good outrage. "See? All you really wanted was my body, after all." She pouted prettily.

"Honey, I already told you once that I wanted to know *you* better, but I've never denied that I was almost crazy in that elevator. If I'd been able to protect you and if you had been coherent, I would have made love to you right there and then," he exclaimed, kissing the tip of her nose and pulling her back down into his arms. "Funnyface and all, honey. *I would have had you!*"

She giggled against his warm hair-matted chest, shaking her head against the picture that had suddenly popped into her head.

"All right, what devilish thought hit you, Ms. Alexander?"

She rolled away from him, hooting with laughter that was fast making her weak.

"Tell me," he ordered gruffly, adding to her dilemma by tickling her to distraction.

"You were sitting right next to five hundred balloons!" she howled, wiping tears from her eyes and trying to wiggle away from Sky's hold.

He fell back and lay stiff and still. "Woman, it's a

good thing I didn't think of that then!" His voice sounded strangled, and Savvy renewed her laughter.

He was just pulling her trembling body into his arms when they heard a car drive up to the house. They listened as the garage door rolled open, then rolled shut, and the car pulled away.

"Hooker's home," Savvy whispered, suddenly alarmed. "I've got to get dressed."

"Nope. Hooker just left again."

"Why would he do that?"

"I left the light on in the garage."

As her muddled brain saw another "light" she pulled from his arms and sat up again. "A signal for privacy, huh? Tell me, does it have a red bulb?" she asked, getting angry at herself for falling for Sky's charms. "I'm surprised you don't have a revolving door in front."

"Simmer down, Savvy," Sky said quietly. "It was Hooker's idea . . . and, if it will set your mind to rest, I've never used it in this house," he added softly. When she refused to speak, he said, "I never thought you'd have me pegged for the celibate life, Savvy. Be fair. I haven't questioned you about your past relationships, have I?"

"No," she admitted, shaking her head. "I suppose I'm just embarrassed. I don't want Hooker to know I've become one of your women."

"I don't have a bunch of women," he countered, stroking her bare back with his fingertips.

"Since when?" she shot back, simultaneously damning her witchy curiosity . . . or was it jealousy?

"Since a month ago. And that's all I'm going to say,"

he answered decisively. "Now are you gonna stay mad or are you going to kiss me?"

His hands had begun to work their magic again on Savvy's sensitized flesh. She turned to smile down at his cute, but not handsome, face. "I'm gonna kiss you, what else?"

"Good!" he exclaimed, taking a deep, relaxing breath as he drew her to him. "And since you think you might be compromised already, let's try some of that 'what else'!"

It was five o'clock in the afternoon before they had their shrimp salad brunch. They ate it in his warm, rumpled bed.

Six

The next two weeks flew by. Savvy was busy every minute of every day because the newspaper article had produced many leads for her business. The Chamber of Commerce asked her to decorate their upcoming banquet, the National Association of Twins accepted her bid to provide the theme for their annual convention to be held the first of the year in Tulsa, and four other large companies gave her the opportunity to submit her ideas for their sales meetings. These major contracts were only the cream of the crop; dozens of single orders for whimsical and creative specialty items were being called in daily.

Savvy enlisted the help of all her friends during this unexpected expansion, but she also had the forethought to begin forming a group of homemakers and retired people for contract work as the business grew and prospered. Many a night she was still awake and working at midnight when Sky came by after his afternoon shift.

"Honey, you've got to get some rest." Savvy leaned back against him as he massaged the tension from her sore shoulder muscles. "Let one of your contract workers fill these balloons with confetti for the Shriners' Gala tomorrow night. I want to take you to bed and love you," he whispered sensuously as his hands started to fondle her unfettered breasts.

She moaned softly at his touch.

"Mmmm, baby, did you plan this?" he asked as he pulled her back into his arms and sank to the thick carpet. "This is a wonderful way to greet me."

She kissed him with lingering longing. "I was hoping to be finished by the time you got off from work, but to be honest, I just never took the time to finish dressing after my shower. Too much work to do." She sighed, still curled against his strong body. "This is my big break, Sky. I can't waste a minute."

Sky almost told her that she was killing herself, but he was quick to squelch his disgruntled feeling. He knew how much the success of her business meant to her. He certainly wasn't going to add to her burden by pouting like a child simply because she wasn't able to find some time for him right now. Instead he offered his help. "Look, honey, I can do this stuff. I'll help you and we can be finished in no time at all. What do you say?"

"But you've worked all day already," she protested, at the same time touched by his offer.

"I have a purely selfish motive," he explained, rubbing his dimpled chin against her flushed cheek. "I'd like a kiss good night before you pass out in my arms. Come on now. Show me what to do."

It took less than an hour to finish the order. Six dozen bright balloons had to have two tablespoons of confetti poured into them before they were filled with helium gas. Savvy showed Sky how to put a little funnel into the specially shaped rubber tubes, easing the confetti through, and then snapping the rubber lip over the gas spigot and filling each to capacity before fastening the end. Soon the mesh nets were bulging with the colored balls and Savvy announced that the job was finished. Exhausted from her eighteen-hour day she left the workroom and fell across her bed. Sky followed and cradled her body against his.

"I'm grateful for your help, Detective Brady." She sighed and snuggled closer. "Tomorrow I'll be moving the operation to a new location. I was able to rent space in a nearby building where my workers and I can spread out and get the larger jobs completed more quickly. I'll just keep the single orders coming from here for the time being," she explained. "I can't be sure if my luck is going to hold with the large assignments . . . but I'm hoping."

She smiled and lifted her face for his kiss. When he covered her mouth with his in a slow, tender expression of longing, Savvy could feel the fatigue and bone-weariness drain from her body. She wanted to show Sky she loved his tenderness and his ability to understand how much she wanted this business to grow.

In fact, she had discovered some days ago that she loved *him*, but she hadn't found the way to tell him yet. Perhaps tonight was the right time.

She lay back against the soft comforter and drew circles in his golden chest curls when he leaned over her. Casually she began to unbutton one button after another until she could smooth her slender fingers over his broad chest. His heart began a thumping parody of his normal beat and she drew him closer and let her lips blaze a pathway where her fingertips had gone. Not saying a word she lifted her mouth to his throat and lingered there for a time before she continued her erotic progress to his jaw and chin, and finally to his waiting parted lips. After a kiss that left them both breathless, Savvy gently pushed Sky's shirt off his shoulders and tossed it carelessly to the floor.

He smiled intriguingly into her heavy-lidded eyes. "You're different tonight, baby. I'm seeing something entirely new." With little effort he removed her knit shirt and bent to kiss her nipples. He was filled with a surge of power when he drew each hard, rounded bud into his mouth. Suddenly he was very grateful that Fate had permitted him his elevator fantasy—her nipples were rosy and smoke-tinted. Someday soon, he promised himself, he would place her feline length upon milky white silk. "Let me do it all tonight, sweetheart," he murmured. "Just lie back and let me make the magic."

She relaxed and allowed her hands to rest at her sides. Sighing contentedly, she smiled her agreement. "Slow and easy?"

"You read my mind, baby," he whispered tremulously.

He rose from her side to turn off the bedside lamp and open the drapes, flooding the room with moonlight. She watched while he pulled off his boots and socks, then he unbuckled his belt and removed the remainder of his clothes. Feeling the heat of his body as he knelt beside her, she tried to help like a sleep-dazed child while he took off the rest of her clothing and lifted her on top of his hard, muscular body. She felt as if she were held within a heavenly cocoon when he parted his legs and bent his knees to cradle her tenderly. His hands began to forage along her spine, bringing life back into her tired limbs. His touch *was* magic, she decided, letting her hips undulate over his fire. When he felt her gyrating heat move against him, Sky chuckled gruffly and moved her back to the bed.

"I said *slow and easy*, honey. That kind of subtle move will get you fireworks!"

"My error," she apologized in a slurred voice. "Carry on." She raised her hand like a queen greeting her subjects.

He chuckled again, soft against her mouth. "My pleasure, honey." The kiss that began as a tender, gentle tribute to her beauty soon deepened. He explored her mouth while his loving fingers skimmed along her silky flesh and targeted her territorial warmth like a heat-sensitive missile intent on its lofty mission. Unthinking, Savvy dropped her hand to his throbbing manhood, subconsciously intent on giving him pleasure and meeting her own need. But he drew away, his breath harsh against her lips. "Don't, baby!

Let me do it all." She did as she was told, uncomplaining and lost to the moment.

He could feel her passion rising. Although she was breathing shallowly and beginning to move against his touch, she was like putty, malleable, pliant, and easily shaped to his liking. Pulling her into his arms, tighter, tighter, he plunged into her secret passage and drove her to a chaotic, sensational climax. When it came, she experienced a star-burst explosion deep within. Her body arched against his hand. She could feel the throbbing grasp of her inner heat wrap around his fingers. Her arms, drained of strength, released their convulsive hold.

His touch gentled, but he continued to circle and probe her ignited femininity with light strokes, coaxing continuous, pleasurable spasms from her center. An eternity passed before it was over.

Sky kissed her moist lips and whispered against her ear. "I'm coming to you now, darling. Slow and easy . . . and long." When he possessed her, Savvy thought she would drown in the whirlpool of her deep love for him. She wanted to say the words, but her lips refused to form the declaration. Instead she let herself drift away beneath his slowly undulating hips as he took her once again to the peaceful side of completion. It was the most wonderful feeling in the world and she sighed in total surrender in his arms. Relaxed and contented beyond her wildest dreams, she fell asleep, curled against Sky's body. She didn't hear him croon with heartfelt sincerity, "I care for you, Savvy. You mean more to me than anyone in the world."

•   •   •

Savvy continued to win bids for banquets and other business functions. She hired a manager and tried to lighten her workload. But she still insisted that she was needed on the premises when a big production was in progress. Her creative talents were being called into use on larger, more complicated projects and her business continued to grow. At three such extravaganzas for national corporations quartered in Tulsa, Sky provided security.

At the first event, Savvy had had nothing to do with his contract; she found out later that a private security firm was part of his plan for the future.

It had been his surprise. "I'm glad you're still with me to share it," he said. Savvy was glad too.

On the second and third assignments, she was asked about providing security and then, of course, she got Sky to work with her. It seemed a match made in heaven. Sky never ventured into her area of expertise or control; she didn't intrude on his authority. The comments and further recommendations from their clients were gratifying. There wasn't one complaint about their combined services. Delighted with their working cooperative, the pair discussed a more permanent business partnership. Savvy suggested they call themselves Secure Entertainment.

Sky's whimsical contribution brought an exasperated frown to her face. "We should be named the Light Tight Delight!"

She snorted in a most unladylike manner. "Sounds more like a massage parlor."

"That's against the law in Tulsa, little lady." He raised a haughty brow and used his condescending detective voice to advantage. "But we could form a private club—just two members—equal partners," he suggested, nuzzling her neck as they cuddled together on her living-room couch. "First we turn out the *light*. Then we love sweet and *tight* to our mutual *delight*! Good idea?"

Any arguments she might have had melted beneath his determined assault. "Maybe we should patent it," she teased, trying to play hard to get.

"Someone beat you to it."

"Oh, yeah? Who?"

"Mother Nature."

Not to be outdone, she had a ready comeback. "I should have guessed it was a *smart woman*."

"One of the smartest things she ever did was to bring us together," he countered, catching her before she wiggled away.

"How so?"

He kissed her with erotic thoroughness and stole Savvy's breath away. "She knew we'd be perfect candidates to keep testing the product. Come here, baby."

It was a long time before he kissed her good night and went home.

Later, after Savvy had just fallen asleep, she was awakened by a phone call. The young woman caller claimed that she had a balloon emergency! One of their company's star salesmen was coming in on a seven A.M. flight from New York and her boss insisted that the man be greeted with a balloon surprise suitable for an up-and-coming winner. Savvy carefully took the flight and billing information from the woman. She had to forego her morning run so she could fill the order and make the delivery. She was fuming when she returned two hours later with the original gift still in her arms. The phone was ringing as she stomped up her stairs to her door.

"Hello!" she shouted into the phone.

"Wow! What side of the bed did you get up on this morning?" It was Sky.

"Oh, it's just awful! I was sent on a wild-goose chase . . . and I'm madder than a whole flock."

"What happened, honey?"

Savvy explained as best she could. Sky immediately thought about Jocko and wondered if he was now trying a new tactic. Sky kept his disquieting thoughts to himself, but he made a silent promise to put a little of the fear of God into Jocko after Savvy ended her explanation. "You know, Sky, I had the strangest feeling that I was being followed."

"Did you notice any car in particular in the morning traffic?" he asked, suddenly very serious.

"There was a souped-up jalopy. Like one of those jumping-bean cars, but it was probably just my imagination. It was weaving in and out of traffic and I was wishing for a motorcycle cop so he could see how they were driving."

"I don't suppose you got a license number?"

" 'Fraid not, Detective Brady. I was so mad I couldn't see straight. I guess I'm going to have to begin calling back on phone orders so this won't happen again. Just another lesson in business."

They discussed a small meeting she had been contracted to do in the evening. "I'll be by to follow you home, Savvy. Don't leave the building until I get there, okay?"

"Hey, Sky-lar," she teased, trying to get him out of

his serious mood. "I was a green belt in karate in college. You don't have to worry about me, buddy."

"I'm more worried about the other guy, *buddy*," he shot back. "And the name is *Sky*. You'll remember that, won't you, darling?" His voice oozed with sex appeal.

"When you ask like that, how can I refuse, sweetheart?" She purred into the phone and heard Sky's low groan of remorse.

"Dirty pool, lady."

"I know." And she gently hung up the receiver, smiling like a Cheshire cat.

That evening her work was completed sooner than she'd expected. Rather than wait until Sky came by, she began to load her equipment and extra supplies herself. It would save time better spent with him, she decided. She pulled her van into the deserted alley so she could save steps as well. Just as she was coming out the door with her last load, a car careened around the corner and screeched to a stop in front of her. The headlights blinded her and she was suddenly afraid to move. The car door slammed shut and she saw the silhouette of a man running toward her. The click of his heels echoed ominously and she was reminded that she was alone and unprotected.

"Dammit, Savvy! You scared the hell out of me!" Sky's booming voice almost knocked her over with its force.

Finding speech, she sputtered back, "*I* scared *you*? I nearly had a heart attack just now. Why didn't you say something?"

Ignoring her cross words he grabbed her arms,

spilling packages onto the bricks. "I thought we agreed that you'd wait inside for me. I went crazy when I couldn't find your van in the parking lot. Then I went in and they told me you were loading up in this alley. Are you nuts?" he croaked. "You could have been mugged or raped . . . or worse."

She realized he was truly terrified for her safety and tried to calm him down. "It's all right, Sky. I haven't been hurt. I was just trying to save some time so we could be together later."

He crushed her in his arms, making it difficult for her to breathe. "I want that too, honey, but not at this price. Don't ever, *ever* do this again. Will you promise?"

"I promise," she said, nearly breathless. "Let's go home. Okay?"

"Don't drive too fast," he ordered, picking up the boxes and putting them in the back of her van.

"In Violet?" Her astonished question brought a cautious smile to Sky's dear face and she hoped he would forgive her.

As she guided her van carefully along the freeway, she could see Sky's car close behind. Tearful over his outburst, she tried to understand why it had happened. She had thought he would be glad not to have to lug all her stuff for her. Then she thought about the evening when they'd had their first dinner together at his home. He had told her about losing his mother and then his grandfather, and finally his father. All in such a short period of time. Could he possibly be thinking that he might lose her? There was so much that he hadn't told her about his past. Had he suffered more terrible losses? Wiping the tears from her cheeks she vowed to be more careful about his secret inner fears, even if she didn't know everything yet.

Sky watched the van in front of him as he drove along. Every few moments he would glance into his rearview mirrors to see if they were being followed. Dammit, he wasn't being paranoid, he told himself. Rumor on the street had it that Jocko had sent out the word. "Put the heat on Brady's lady clown. I don't want her at the trial."

Sure, Sky could "talk" to Jocko in his own language, but he still had no proof of harassment. And he didn't want to scare Savvy to death either. But it was damn hard walking this tightrope between judicious caution and outright stupidity, he thought, getting mad all over again at Savvy's foolish behavior.

God, I don't want to lose her, he prayed. *Please watch over her when I'm not near. I love her.*

They kissed and made up that night, both apologizing for making the other angry. The next morning and every morning that week, Sky was waiting for her when she went out for her morning run. She had told him that her friend Teri had gone away on a business trip and he volunteered to run with her. Just to keep her company, he said. But Savvy suspected that he was worried about her . . . and she didn't want him to have to worry about her. She'd be just fine. If only he could tell her what was bothering him, she thought sadly. He said someday. Would that day ever come?

Seven

Sky invited Savvy to his ranch on Saturday. It was time for her to see his home, he said. Savvy would have moved heaven and earth to accept and she almost did! When they pulled away from her apartment that morning she was silently blessing her new manager. The woman had raised seven children and Savvy felt sure she could keep everything moving smoothly for a day.

Outside of Bartlesville they stopped for breakfast at a quaint German restaurant built like a windmill. Inside, the decor was beautifully authentic. Blue and white tiles trimmed the freestanding fireplace. The walls were paneled, and Dresden plates were balanced along a high shelf that ran above the lace-curtained windows. A peasant-costumed waitress served them heavy potato pancakes and homemade sausages with spicy, coarse applesauce and mugs of steaming coffee. Familiar strains of Bach and Wagner filled the room. When Sky and Savvy rose to leave, feeling replete and satisfied, the manager bid them farewell in German. It was a lovely gesture.

After another half-hour's drive along back-country roads—Sky swore it was a shortcut to his ranch—they arrived at the homestead. It was everything Savvy could have imagined. The house was delightful. Victorian gingerbread trimmed every peak and gable. The white picket fence was the final, perfect touch. After she had gone inside to meet Mr. and Mrs. Jablonski, Sky took her on a tour of his home, which was filled with many antiques dating back to his great-grandfather's day.

"It's time for our picnic, pretty lady," Sky announced, dragging Savvy along through the kitchen, where he picked up a pair of packed saddlebags and smacked a thank-you kiss on Mrs. Jablonski's cheek. Savvy barely had time to wave good-bye before he dragged her out the door to the saddled quarter horses tied to the hitching post by the back door.

Savvy dug in her heels and skidded to a stop. "How do you know I can ride? You never bothered to ask me, Brady."

A shocked look came over Sky's face. "You can, can't you?"

She hid her smile and answered softly. "A little."

This was too good to pass up, she decided. After following him around all morning, never being allowed to tarry long at any interesting object in the home, she was going to have some fun. It seemed as if he had been eager to leave the house almost from the moment they got there.

He smiled affectionately and helped her into the saddle. "We'll go slow, honey. I just assumed you'd know how to ride if your parents raised horses. You're not afraid, are you?"

"A little," she answered again in her softest, most feminine voice.

"I'll take care of you, baby. Don't worry about a thing." After he had tied on the saddlebags, he swung up into his saddle and led the way from the yard. He kept glancing over at his charge, still finding it difficult to believe her story.

"Which way are we going?" she asked once they were out on the road, crossing over to the prairie beyond.

"Straight ahead for about two miles," he answered, leaning over to adjust the reins along the side of his horse's head.

That moment was all she needed. She let out a holler that would have raised the dead and dug her heels into her horse's flanks as she settled into the saddle for a wild ride. She leaned into the wind, feeling it tear at her blond curls and whip her blouse flat against her chest. "Come on, girl. Let's show Sky-lar what we know about riding." She urged the horse faster and laughed with exultation as she flew across the flatland to the first rise.

She glanced back and saw that Sky was closing in

fast. She could hear his warning on the wind. "You little sneak. Wait till I get my hands on you. You're not going to be able to sit down for a week," he promised, laughing in spite of his outrage at her fast-thinking dirty trick. And at his expense too!

When she approached the second gentle rise, the land looked somehow familiar to her. She knew she had never been there before but she gazed with searching eyes as if she would find some landmark to confirm her unknown knowledge. Then she saw it. One hundred yards ahead was a lone old oak tree, spreading its leafy limbs to provide shade for a weary traveler . . . or a frightened clown. She reined in her horse and sat quietly, looking over the meadow dotted with bluebells and black-eyed Susans. This was the secret place Sky had taken her to in her mind while they were trapped together in the elevator. Tears of gratitude misted her vision and the land and sky swam together in an Impressionistic painting of her memory. The place was *real*. And it belonged to her love.

Sky came up beside her, saying nothing. Silently they rode to the tree, then slid from their saddles and dropped the reins. The horses began to munch on the tender meadow grasses and Savvy and Sky walked arm in arm to sit beneath the gnarled oak.

He kissed her tenderly as they sank to the soft earth. "I've never brought another woman to this spot, Savvy. It's been my secret place for as long as I can remember. But I wanted you to see it. I wanted to be here when I told you that I love you." He caught her face between his large, rough hands and kissed her again with a gentleness that bespoke his feeling for her. "I love you with all my heart, Savvy." Their eyes met and she could tell how much he loved her. She smiled radiantly, knowing the moment had come when she could tell him of her love. But when she parted her lips to speak he stopped her. "Don't say it unless you mean it, honey. I couldn't stand it if you ever left me. I want you to be my wife."

He seemed more vulnerable than she had ever seen him and finally guessed the reason. "Someone else didn't keep her word?"

A frown of conflict crossed his forehead, then he sighed and leaned back against the tree trunk, his decision made. "It's happened twice before as a matter of fact," he answered gruffly.

"Can you tell me about it?" Hoping to ease his pain she stroked his cheek and leaned against him. Both looked out over the quiet, tranquil meadow for long moments before Sky found the courage to tell her everything.

"The first time was when I was overseas. I had been going steady with a girl in high school and we planned to marry when I got out. I received the typical 'Dear John' letter. She married some Mexican millionaire's son."

"But you were already rich!"

"Yeah, but I wasn't there." He laughed harshly. "Hooker never liked her. I should have listened to him. Anyway, the last I heard she was on her fourth husband, each one a little richer and a little dumber than the last."

"That's awful. What did you do when you got the letter so far from home?"

"I was in a fog for days," he answered glumly. "The

ambush hit right after that. It blew me right out of the water. Everyone was killed except Hooker and me. The whole patrol wiped out. My friends . . . my responsibility . . ." His voice drifted away in painful memories.

"Is that why you say your scars don't show?" She had taken his hand in hers and was holding it to her heart.

"I didn't get a scratch. But it was months before I healed. And sometimes, like now, it still hurts like hell."

They sat quietly, both caught up in their own thoughts. "You said it had happened twice, Sky."

He pulled himself straighter and began to speak again in a low monotone. "Three years ago I almost married a woman I didn't love. You see, by that time I'd decided that love wasn't for me. I'd lost too many people I loved. It hurt too much to lose. In a way, she shared my feelings. We respected one another and were compatible, but there wasn't any fire between us. We were just going to go it together." He sighed with disgust. "Hooker told me I was crazy. I think he might have expressed the same opinion to my fiancée. At any rate, the end of the story is that she accepted a big promotion in her company and told me 'no hard feelings' the day before she flew off to New York City. I sold the ring and went to Florida for a week," he said with a flush of embarrassment. "All I got out of it was a blasted sunburn!"

"You must have been terribly hurt, Sky. I don't know if I could have pulled myself back together again."

He laughed and his tone was lighter this time.

"Ironically, I was mostly kicking myself for being a fool. I didn't have any real feelings for the woman I was going to marry. We just thought it would be a convenient partnership so we wouldn't have to be alone. I thought I'd learned my lesson. Love wasn't for me; I couldn't trust my heart. It hurt too damn bad when I lost. And you know how much I need to win, Savvy."

"Is that the end of your story?" she asked in a small, quavering voice.

He pulled her tighter against him. "Yeah," he whispered against her wind-tossed silky hair. "I thought I was doing just fine until I was ambushed again . . . by a scared bit of heaven in a crazy clown suit. I *do* love you, baby."

She turned in his arms and searched his serious face, reading his love in eyes that were sincere and a little afraid too. She understood so much now. His reason for pulling back, for holding back his trust; his vulnerabilities and fear of losing her once he'd declared his love for her. Her heart nearly leaped from her breast as she whispered the words she'd been longing to say. "I love you, Sky Brady. I want to spend the rest of my life with you. I want to be your wife and the mother of your children. I love *you* . . . only you."

"Oh, sweetheart, don't ever leave me. This time I'd die. I'll need you for the rest of my days . . . and nights."

Together they lay down in the sweet meadow grasses, feeling the breeze caress their skin as they made tender love to bind their commitment to one another for life. Afterward as they spoke quietly of plans for their future, Sky withdrew a tiny package wrapped in white tissue from his pants pocket. He placed it lovingly in her palm. Inside was an old-fashioned engagement ring made from platinum in a basket design and set with a single large sparkling diamond. "This was my mother's ring, honey. I'd like you to have it now. There'll never be another woman more perfect for me."

With tears in her eyes, she watched as he slipped the ring onto her finger and sealed his promise by kissing the shimmering stone. Her misted vision revealed a thousand prisms of rainbow splendor around his bowed head.

All during the next day while she worked alone in her home office Savvy continually admired her engagement ring. She felt happier than she had ever dreamed possible. That morning she had called home and told her parents that she was in love and was going to marry a wonderful man. At first they were surprised at her announcement, but when she promised to bring him home to meet them the first free weekend, her mother and dad calmed down enough to ask many, many questions about their future son-in-law. She laughed aloud when she remembered their parting words. "We know you, Savena. When you make up your mind, it stays made up. If you love him, we know we will too. Just promise us you won't elope." She gave her solemn promise and bid them good-bye, but not before all three said, "I love you." No daughter had better parents, she decided thankfully.

Her bright outlook on life continued until four in the afternoon. She had just stopped work to put together an intimate dinner for two. Sky would be over shortly; he had covered for one of his friends on the force on his second day off because the man wanted to attend his grandchild's christening. When the phone rang she ran to answer it, thinking it must be her future husband. Instead she heard a gruff, disguised voice.

"You're gonna be the saddest clown in Tulsa if you testify against Jocko." Then the receiver was slammed down with an explosive bang. She stood frozen, staring at the phone as if it had suddenly turned into a viper ready to strike her dead. The click and ominous buzz of the disconnected line made her jump in terror. Trembling, she hung up the phone.

Trancelike she walked back into the kitchen and began tearing lettuce for a salad. The impact of the threatening words finally reached her brain and she began to cry. "What am I going to do?" she asked the empty room. "I can't tell Sky. He'll be so upset, he'll do something crazy . . . anything to protect me." No, she told herself, trying to calm down. She wouldn't say anything. She'd just be very, very careful until the trial was over. No cheap thug was going to scare her. She almost believed her brave words.

Sky arrived an hour later and when he greeted her with a kiss, she moved against him with a passion founded on fear. He moaned happily when she kissed him again and again, trying desperately to give him more love than he had ever known.

"Fantastic, pretty lady! Can I count on a homecoming like this for the rest of my life?"

"Every night for the rest of our lives, darling!" And she kissed him again to show what she meant.

During dinner the phone rang again. She jumped as if she'd been struck by lightning. Sky offered to answer it, but she leaped up and mumbled something about expecting a call from Teri. "Hello?" She listened for a moment. "No, I'm sorry, but you have the wrong number." When she replaced the receiver her face was drained of its color. The same voice had another message. "Don't think Brady can protect you, you bitch. We can get you anytime we want."

She rummaged around in the refrigerator for a long time before she had herself under firm enough control to return to the table. When she sat down again Sky watched her movements closely. "Who was on the phone, Savvy?" His voice was low and alert.

She laughed nervously and fluttered her hands in a jerky gesture. "You heard, honey. It was a wrong number." His momentary frown worried her more than the caller. How was she going to keep this from Sky so he wouldn't do something crazy? When the phone rang a second time, he pushed her firmly back into her chair and rose to his feet.

"I'll get it this time, Savvy. You finish your dessert." He walked to the ringing instrument and picked it up. Savvy could feel the controlled violence in his movement. "Detective Brady here. Who's calling?" He spoke with all the authority he was able to muster in his harsh voice. He pulled the phone from his ear; Savvy could hear the loud click all the way in the living room. "The punk hung up," he exploded, slamming the phone down.

He returned to the table and sat down, then pinned her with his laser blue stare. "Have you been bothered by unwanted calls?" he asked carefully. He didn't want to use the word "threatening" if he didn't have to. Frightening her to death was not what he had in mind. He only wanted to protect her . . . especially if Jocko had started a new line of harassment.

She tried to smile but wasn't very successful. "If you must know, I had a call earlier. No one talked to me," she lied. "They just hung up in my ear." She mustered a small laugh. "It's probably just some unattended kids having a little fun at my expense," she said as reasonably as she was able.

"Are you sure, Savvy?" He never took his eyes from her pale features. "I want you to tell me if you've been frightened by these calls. You can trust me to take care of it, baby."

She shut her eyes momentarily against the horrible scene that had leaped to mind. She couldn't take the chance on telling Sky the truth. He might get himself hurt . . . or killed! When she opened her eyes he was still frowning at her. "I'd tell you if I were afraid, Sky. Honestly, I would. It's just some kids playing with the damn phone, that's all," she repeated. "Don't worry about it. Okay?" She rose to begin clearing the dishes, but he caught her around the waist and pulled her into his lap.

Kissing her hungrily, he tried to show her how much he cared. "I'll always worry about you, honey. I need you like I need breath for life."

"And I need you, my love," she murmured.

When he left a little later Savvy was unable to tell if she had really convinced him about the phone calls. For that matter he had been rather distant, so that she was now worried that he doubted her love. What could she do to prove her feelings? she wondered in anguish. He needed more assurance than most men. He'd lost so much already. After an hour of tossing and turning in her bed, she finally fell asleep with a smile on her face. She had a plan and she would put it into action tomorrow.

When Sky called the following morning to check on her, he convinced her that she should take the day off and get some rest. He was thinking that she'd be safer off the streets until he could check out his informants. Something was definitely going down and he wanted to make sure Savvy didn't get in the way. He also wanted to call in some favors from his buddies on the force. After a mild confrontation of wills, Savvy gave her promise, but she smiled as she gave it. She had planned to stay home anyway. She needed to prepare for Sky's arrival that night.

"Will you be here right after your shift tonight, sweetheart?" She purred as sweetly as any kitten.

"Wild horses couldn't keep me away, honey."

All day long she worked on her surprise. After Sky called during his dinner break, promising to see her as soon as he could, she treated herself to a warm bubble bath. She was extravagant with the perfumed beads and luxuriated in the frothy liquid until she was rested and relaxed. Then she smoothed fragrant lotion over every inch of her body and brushed her clean hair until it was a wild mass of silken curls. Pulling all the drapes, she lit one candle in her living room and sat down on the floor in a meditative position to await his arrival. The candlelight made dancing patterns on the shadowed walls and illuminated in its gentle glow the breathtaking loveliness of Savvy's sensual nude body. She concentrated on her exciting adventure with her loved one, her man for all time. Every cell in her being was alert yet tranquil.

When she heard the familiar sound of his sports car pulling into the parking lot and the slam of his car door, she rose in one graceful movement, listening for his footsteps on her stairs. When he paused at her door, she glided to her bedroom and shut the door. All was ready. This was to be her proof to him.

Outside Sky stood in the circle of light from the overhead bulb. He leaned forward to read the note taped to Savvy's door, at the same time fumbling in his pocket for the duplicate key she had given him the week before. He puzzled over her message, wondering what in the devil she was up to now.

"Detective Skylar Brady," it read. "Enter at your own risk. The occupant is armed and should be considered dangerous."

He chuckled softly as he fit the key into the lock and opened the door. He had no idea what to expect. Candlelight and complete silence were what greeted him when he entered. Where the hell was she? he mused. He glanced down and spotted a construction-paper yellow brick road leading to her closed bedroom door. Calling her name softly, he paused for a moment to put his service revolver into the kitchen drawer before following the path. "Savvy? Where are you, love? I'd rather play something a bit more grown-up than hide and seek, honey." He got no answer, not even a little giggle to signal her hiding place.

Shrugging, he made his way to the bedroom. On the door was taped another important-looking message. He pulled out his lighter and read it with growing delight. "Detective Brady: Do not enter . . . unless you are prepared to search out the suspect. She is guilty of only one thing. She loves you! Caution: Take off your boots, step lightly, and lock the door behind you. Savvy?"

His heart began to hammer in anticipation. Solving this mystery might be one of the most interesting and exciting bits of detective work of his career, he decided. He pulled off his boots, then pushed open the door and entered Savvy's bedroom. At once he was aware of two things. One: It was pitch-black in her room. And two: He was standing in a sea of bobbing balloons! When he reached out, he touched balloons; when he raised his arms, he felt nothing but floating, air-light balls as high as he could stretch. *"Ver-y in-ter-r-resting!"* he said in a wicked, leering voice. He listened intently, hoping to hear one little sound that would pinpoint Savvy's location. Hearing nothing, he began to wade around the room, using his arms like a swimmer to breaststroke through the undulating mass. He reached the bed and explored every inch, but found no Savvy. He tried to be very scientific about it, gridding the room in his imagination and searching each section methodically. No Savvy. He began to lose patience and swore when he stubbed his toe on her dresser. He heard the tiniest giggle from the corner of the room and zeroed in on the sound. What he found was the closed closet door. He knew he wouldn't find her hiding in there. She still had to fight the residual terror from her childhood entrapment. But since there was nowhere else to search, he opened the door cautiously and stepped inside, whispering, "Savvy?"

"Freeze, Detective Brady. I've got you covered." Intrigued, he didn't move a muscle. Gentle hands pushed aside his jacket and slid it from his broad shoulders to the floor. Competent fingers slowly unknotted his tie and drew it from around his neck. He could feel the material slip and slide; it was an erotic sensation. Still complying with her throaty instructions, he stood frozen to the spot until a warm, soft body pressed boldly against him. Instantly he became intoxicated with her perfume and lifted his leaden arms to enfold her. He sucked in his breath in white-hot desire when he touched her. She felt satiny smooth. She felt soft and trembly. And she was filled with a matching flame in every pulsating cell of her naked body. He began the low keening sound that signaled his churning passion as he stroked her skin, almost out of control.

"I warned you that I was armed and should be considered dangerous," she whispered a moment before she captured his lips in a sizzling, tempestuous kiss that rocked him to his toes.

Gasping for breath, he could only wheeze a feeble comeback. "And me without a weapon."

She laughed with delight, and the sensuous sound insinuated itself directly into his marrow. "Oh, I don't know about that!" She discarded his clothes with dazzling dispatch. When he was as naked as she, Savvy began a serious assault upon his flesh, kissing and caressing him with more intimacy than she'd ever dared before. "No, Brady. I think your assumption is all wrong. You *are* armed . . . with one of the most lethal weapons known to womankind," she said, feeling the throb of his powerful manhood beneath her touch.

Finding just a small portion in his dwindling reservoir of control, he asked one question and was surprised at the breaking quality in his voice. "Why are we making love in the dark . . . in your closet, when we could be on your king-sized bed floating in a cloud of balloons?"

She hugged him so tight he could barely catch his breath. Her nakedness rubbing against his bare skin didn't help in the least. "This was the closest thing I could think of to a stuck elevator. Don't you see, darling? My confidence in you has cured my claustrophobia. I'm not afraid anymore of the dark or closed places . . . or you."

"Of me?" He choked, suddenly afraid again.

"Well, my attraction and love for you."

"And now?"

"I love you." Her words vibrated against his parted lips.

He hated himself for asking, but his fear had taken him by surprise. "For how long?"

She recognized his vulnerability and answered him with all the love in her heart. "Forever, my love."

"Forever is a long time."

"And I don't want to waste a minute." Before she could kiss him again, he lifted her high in his arms and walked—with great care—through the fantasy world of an undulating helium sea to her bed. There, on waves of passion, he took her with him above it all until they burst in wonder upon an ocean of swirling stars. As they rode the crest and then rested among the calming waters of completion, Sky lay entwined with his most perfect love. His Savvy.

Eight

After that night of love and true understanding Sky was amazed at the change in the world around him. Suddenly he found himself in a place filled with hope where once there had been ugliness and despair. His job seemed less burdensome; his worries and concerns almost nonexistent. He took a long walk on his property the next morning and was so taken by the beauty around him that he was virtually overcome with emotion. At long last the woman in all his dreams had convinced him of her undying love for him. She'd recognized qualities in him that he had almost lost touch with . . . creativeness, affection, and a desire to reach out to people. "Because of Savvy I'm alive again," he shouted to the sky. "Oh, thank you for letting her love me."

Savvy awoke with a dreamy smile on her well-kissed lips. "He loves me," she crooned, lifting her hand so the sunlight reflected in her engagement ring. "And I love him with all my heart." She rolled over onto the other pillow and buried her face against the smooth case. Breathing deeply she recognized the subtle essence of the man with whom she was going to share her life. Cuddling closer into the soft headrest, she grew philosophical. It seemed a miracle to her that she'd found another person who was dear to her and who had magnified her joy for life and her desire to give herself to whatever their life together offered. "I should have known from the first moment I met him," she said with conviction. "Something in my universe went click!" Delighted at her wise and truthful observation, she filled the room with peals of joyful, melodic laughter. Nothing could go wrong now.

All through the week their friends and business associates congratulated them on their engagement. Teri cried when Savvy asked her to be her maid of honor. "He *is* the one for you," she exclaimed, hugging her friend and dripping tears all over Savvy.

When Sky made the announcement to Hooker and asked him to be his best man, Hooker almost broke his hand pounding Sky on the back. Savvy was there, too, and she didn't think her rib cage would ever be the same again after the bear hug he delivered. His burst of rejoicing finished, he immediately began plans for an intimate dinner party to be given on Friday evening to celebrate.

"There will be six of us, I think. Jake and Maggie, the newly betrothed couple, the bride's maid of honor, and the groom's *best man.* I should fill the bill nicely, don't you think?" Sky and Savvy both agreed with him because he was gadding about like a proud peacock at the time. "Is Teri a foxy lady?" he asked, his dark eyes sparking with interest.

"A true vixen," Savvy answered solemnly. "You'll love her."

Winking mischievously, he said, "I always do, Savvy, darlin'. I always do!"

Contracts for large meetings and banquets continued to pour into Savvy's office. Each one requested that her company provide security in addition to her usual services. After a long private discussion, Savvy and Sky decided to incorporate. They made arrangements to meet with his attorney, his accountant, and his tax specialist on Thursday morning. After a meeting that lasted four hours, Savvy and Sky signed the final papers that teamed them up into one business organization—Secure Entertainment. Savvy had made Sky promise beforehand that he wouldn't even bring up his suggestion for a name in jest! This was serious business, she had admonished him when he continued to tease her about it.

At the meeting Sky put into motion a plan for their corporation to purchase and remodel the existing building where Savvy had rented space. "We're going to need it for a tax write-off, honey," he explained when she grew wide-eyed and alarmed at the asking price. "Don't worry. I've got the money. And we're going to make a whole lot more by the looks of things."

His staff of experts nodded in total agreement so Savvy was forced to throw up her hands and look at the light side. "That's what I say, partner. *Let's go for it!*"

"My exact sentiments, darling," he replied drolly. Then he kissed her right in front of everyone and no one batted an eye!

By Thursday evening they were exhausted from their whirlwind day. So much had been accomplished and everything had gone along as smooth as silk, except that Savvy felt a little queasy. Was she coming down with the flu? she wondered.

"Can you stand a little more news, Savvy?" Sky was holding her in his arms on the couch where they had both collapsed after dinner.

"You brought in another oil well!"

"Better than that . . . I think."

She sat up and turned her flushed face to his, kissing his nose and cheeks and growling as she climbed into his lap, then nipped at his ear. "You brought in *two* oil wells?" The suspense was no doubt causing that little twinge of discomfort in her side, she decided. Calm down, she lectured herself, and absentmindedly massaged the tense, constricting muscles.

"I gave my notice," Sky said. "After two weeks while I take my vacation time, I'll be a former member of Tulsa's Finest."

Her mouth dropped open in shock, the pain in her side forgotten for the moment. She was having difficulty assimilating his announcement. "You mean it? You're leaving the police department?"

He nodded, never breaking contact with her wide, startled stare. He was watching her, hoping it was the right decision. When her expressive eyes began to shine with gathering tears, he still wasn't certain what her reaction was going to be. But then she threw her arms around him and hugged and kissed him as if he had been lost and suddenly found after years of separation.

"Oh, my God!" She kissed him again and again. Her tears of happiness wet his cheeks. "Oh, Sky, I can't believe it. It's an answer to my dreams. You're going to be safe. I won't have to be sick with worry every time you go on duty." Unconsciously she cradled her damp palm against the nagging abdominal ache.

"I had no idea that you worried about me that much." His look of astonishment sobered Savvy's rejoicing instantly.

"Oh, darling, perhaps you're acting too hastily." She furtively wiped her eyes and tried to express her thoughts. "I don't want you to quit the force if it's going to make you unhappy. Honestly, Sky. I'd never ask you to do it."

Smiling bemusedly, Sky gathered Savvy into his arms and hugged her tight. Unknowingly his warm body assuaged the insistent spasm. "I know you wouldn't ask me, honey. But that step was a part of my tentative plans for the future even before I met you. Our new partnership just accelerated progress, that's all," he explained.

He sighed happily when he slipped his hand

beneath her oversized sweatshirt and caressed her firm, thrusting breasts. Feeling her nipples come alive in his palm, he pushed aside her shirt and drew a bud into his hot mouth. "Oh, baby, my plans for our pleasure are accelerating by leaps and bounds . . . right now! Let's celebrate."

Moaning her compliance to his delicious suggestion, she ignored the soreness below her waist and slid down into the softness of the couch. She drew him over her body, wanting nothing more at the moment than to express all the love she was feeling for her beloved Sky. He moved against her with a mastery that made her go limp with longing. She knew she would never ever tire of his expert love-making. If she lived to one hundred—and she hoped she did!—life with Sky Brady would never be boring. She promised herself that she would always appreciate him, would never let a day or night go by without telling him how much she loved him, and would show him in a million ways how much she cherished him. She reminded herself again, as she began to mirror Sky's tender caresses, that this man needed assurance of her continuing love and devotion more than many men. His need would take top priority in her life's goals. Listening to his murmured phrases of sweet love and commitment, she knew she would always be his top priority as well. And who in her right mind could ask for more? she mused, following as he began leading her toward another glorious private chapter of their lives together.

The strident ringing of the phone intruded upon their journey. "Let it ring, Savvy," Sky pleaded as he renewed his efforts to convince her. "Nothing's more important than this, love."

Savvy couldn't agree with him more. She was relieved when the ringing stopped. But then it immediately began to send out another clamorous signal. "They're not going to give up, Sky." Rolling out from under his aroused body she padded to the phone, massaging the catch in her side and chuckling softly at Sky's grumbling in the background. "Hello? Yes, he's here. Just a moment, please." She held the receiver out to Sky. "It's for you. I think it's your partner."

Sky barreled to his feet and crossed the room in four agitated strides. "Jake? Yeah. What the hell do you want that couldn't have waited?" He scowled when he heard Savvy's maternal clucking behind his back, but his face smoothed with desire as he watched her lie back down on the couch, bare to her waist, waiting for his speedy return.

Suddenly alert, he snapped his head up and said into the phone, "What? What did you say? Tell it again . . . and dammit, take your time, Connelly." He listened attentively, his frown growing more and more pronounced. "Yeah. Yeah. When? . . . Who did it? . . . Damn, I wish it hadn't happened like this. . . . Well, I guess that closes the case no matter how you look at it." He sighed, took in a great breath of air, then let it out on another exasperated sigh. "Thanks for telling me, Jake. We'll see you tomorrow night. Yeah. So long." He hung up the receiver and stood looking out the glass door, seeing nothing, lost in thought.

"What was that all about, Sky?" The room had suddenly chilled and Savvy drew her shirt over her head and smoothed it along her unfulfilled breasts. "Bad news?"

Sky pulled himself back to the present and collapsed beside Savvy. "Yes and no," he answered, still frowning. "Jocko's dead."

The air around them crackled with the static of shock and the need to know more. Savvy gave Sky her undivided attention, but she wished these sharp pains would stop. They were getting worse.

"He's dead." Sky slammed his fist into the other palm. "Dammit, that little hood got himself killed." As he explained the circumstances to her, he grew more and more upset. "Somehow or other one of his sidekicks got a switchblade smuggled in to him. The guy who shared his cell started to give Jocko some lip. Probably began riding him about his ability to lead when he was locked up in jail. Anyway Jocko pulled his blade, but the other guy was a little stronger and a little meaner. He took the knife away and cut him, bad. As soon as the guard heard the fight he tried to break it up, but he was too late. They rushed Jocko to the hospital, but they couldn't save him. He died an hour ago." Sky fell silent and Savvy took his hand and tried to uncoil his fingers from the hard fist. She was hurting both mentally and physically and had to wait for a minute before she could speak.

"You didn't have anything to do with his death, Sky. It's just one of those awful things you won't have to think about anymore, darling."

His reaction to her soothing words was absolutely counter to what she might have expected. He bolted from the couch and began pacing like a caged jungle cat. "I might have had more to do with it than you think, Savvy. I've been riding the hell out of him. Warning him against harassing you. You didn't fool me about those phone calls," he told her. He watched her wince and lean forward, wrapping her arms tightly around her middle. "It didn't take much for Jocko to admit he was responsible, but then again, it didn't take much to convince him to stop!"

He laughed in disgust. "A real winner, was Jocko the Blade. He was the one who sent you on that wild-goose chase to the airport a few weeks ago too. And now he'll never stand trial for the purse-snatching. I can't figure out my feelings, Savvy," he lamented harshly. "Part of me is feeling cheated because he didn't live to the trial; the rest of me is relieved that I don't have to worry about your safety concerning him."

"I wasn't worried, Sky." Savvy rose slowly and walked to his side. She tried to hold him, but he slipped away from her and turned to her with eyes blazing, a distorted look of fear marring his good looks. His wild stare overlooked her feverish gaze and the pinched chalk-white expression around her tight, dry lips.

"Savvy, you don't understand, do you? Let me spell it out for you, babe. Word on the street was, get Brady's lady! Can't you see how that affected me? I would have died before I let that creep hurt you. I pulled in every favor owed me from the people on the force. You haven't been out of sight of a police officer since this thing broke. Except when you were with me."

Savvy sank back down on the couch; it was suddenly intolerable to stand. Nevertheless she was impressed with the degree of his fear for her. With his history of losing people he loved, was it any wonder that he would react so harshly to a threat to her? But how could she relieve his fear? Hoping to help him in any way she could, she lifted her ashen face and tried to smile. "We won't have to worry about that anymore, sweetheart." Her voice was hushed and low. "You've already given your resignation to the police department. Everything is going to be all right now."

She watched in silent agony as his expressive features twisted. "But I'll still be in the security field," he replied. "And you'll soon be the wife of a very rich man. Millionaires and their wives and children are prime targets for kidnappers." His voice broke with emotion. "I don't know if you should take the risk, baby." His words drifted into space and time as he gazed again out the glass door. "I don't know if I want you to. I couldn't stand it if anything happened to you."

Tears of indecision and remorse glistened in his eyes. He blinked repeatedly to hold back this ultimate expression of his vulnerability. Except for Hooker's and Jake's friendship, hadn't Fate snatched away every loving relationship he'd ever cherished and nurtured? he asked himself in sorrow. Why should his everlasting love for Savvy be an exception to Brady's Rule? Maybe he was jinxed for life. Maybe he had been right in the first place, he thought sadly. Love wasn't supposed to be a part of his existence . . . not in this lifetime anyway.

Savvy tried once more to bring him out of his

depression. She'd do whatever she could to help this man she loved. "We'll make it together, Sky. Don't think about your past disappointments, darling. Think about the future. *Our future*. We need one another."

Sky took Savvy into his arms and crushed her against him. It felt as if he were trying to pull her inside his flesh. He shut his eyes to the frightening scenes that kept repeating in his brain and knew he had to leave. He had to get things into perspective. He had to think.

"Look, baby," he began in a controlled, reasonable voice, "I just remembered that I promised Hooker I'd pick up his order from the liquor store tonight. He'll have ten kinds of fits if I don't do it." He laughed confidently and hugged her again, keeping her close so she couldn't read the suppressed terror still shadowing his eyes. "After all, the party is in our honor. I'd better get it done before they close. Okay?"

Suddenly afraid to let him out of her sight, she said, "I'll come along with you."

Sky just gave her another bone-crushing hug, causing Savvy to gasp both from fear and an excruciating stab of pain. He forced himself to chuckle softly against her hair. "No, honey," he answered quickly. Perhaps too quickly. "I'll do it. You just stay here and begin all those marvelous feminine preparations on that gorgeous body of yours. You need to relax a little anyway. You look drained."

Savvy was trying desperately to read his thoughts. Her mind was whirling. She was going to lose him, cried her terrified heart. Simultaneously, her stomach was churning in knotted protest. Swallowing hard, she tried to hold back her tears and control the twisting knife-pain in her belly. In a minute she was going to be sick. "Will you be back tonight?" she asked.

He hesitated for a second, silently interpreting her pale, drawn features. Then he kissed her as if he'd never see her again. "Wild horses couldn't keep me away, baby." His masculine growl was meant to convince her. It seemed to do the trick for she stood quietly in his embrace and caressed him in a way that would make him hurry back to her bed.

"I'll hold you to it, Brady. We have some unfinished business if I'm not mistaken." She tried to make her words sound coquettish, but her voice wavered, almost out of control.

He tipped her chin up and kissed her on the tip of her pert nose. "It'll be my pleasure, ma'am," he assured her, hesitating for a moment before he whispered softly, "So long, honey."

When he turned to leave, the impact of her first intuition—she would not see him again—hit her with the force of a pole ax . . . straight into her breaking heart. The pain radiated across her chest and caused the aching fireball in her side to explode with excruciating intensity. She felt as if a giant fist had been hooked into her body and she doubled over, crying. "Sky! Oh, God, Sky!"

Whirling, terror-stricken, Sky rushed to her. He held her hunched-over body as she tried to stagger to the bathroom. "Savvy, what is it? What's wrong?"

"Bathroom. Please. Going to be sick." She made it to the sink a second before her stomach convulsed and emptied itself. The white-hot, tormenting stabs increased until they were a constant condition and she began to collapse, but Sky's arms held her in a careful embrace. "Something's terribly wrong," she said, gasping. "I can't stand up. The pain's so bad."

"Where, Savvy? Where's the pain?" His features were contorted; he was trying to absorb her pain.

"In my side." She choked, groaning. "It started like a stomach flu, but it's gotten much worse and now it's in my side. Oh, God, Sky! Could I be having an attack of appendicitis?" She had to stop speaking when she was hit with dry heaves; there was nothing more inside her. The shock of his final departure had siphoned off her last bit of strength.

Grabbing a washcloth, Sky solicitously bathed her flushed face and white-edged mouth. Then he swept her into his strong arms, snatching a towel for her to hold in case she got another convulsive attack, and carried her to her bed. He noted the glazed condition of her pain-filled eyes when he lay her down. She wasn't able to lie on her back and had to turn onto her side, curling up and holding her middle. Before he could say a word Savvy's trembling hand snaked out and coiled around his fingers.

"Don't leave me, Sky. Please. Not until the pain goes away," she begged frantically. Huge crystal tears rolled from her eyes and she couldn't have said if they were caused by the burning pain in her body or the wretched beat of her dying heart.

"I won't leave you, honey," he promised softly. "But we've got to get some help for you. I'm calling an ambulance to take you to the hospital." Unable and unwilling to break from her iron hold, Sky picked up the phone with his left hand and dialed 911.

Savvy was barely aware of the roaring engine and the blaring siren as the ambulance hurtled along the streets to the hospital. Withdrawing against the constant gnawing pain, she only knew Sky was nearby, trying desperately to ease the gripping pressure with soft, encouraging words and gentle caresses to her tangled hair and damp cheeks. When she cried out with a sudden stab of pain, her dazed mind registered his shout to the driver.

"Damn it, man! Move this bucket of bolts!"

Slipping into a warm cocoon of unconsciousness she silently commended Sky's order and vaguely felt the surge of increased speed. Her thinking processes were muddled but she was convinced of one thing. Detective Sky Brady was a man to be reckoned with during an emergency.

Nine

Savvy's body was wracked by flame-streaked torment. Her mind was disoriented, but she was aware of the hurried jostling of the paramedics when they wheeled her gurney through the doors of the hospital emergency entrance. Once inside a tiny curtained cubicle a nurse drew blood while a doctor gently palpated Savvy's distended, tender stomach.

"I'm Detective Sky Brady, Second District," she heard Sky say. "This woman is Savena Alexander. She's a personal friend so don't try to kick me out of here." He clasped Savvy's limp hand in his strong, warm grip. "I won't get in the way . . . but *I'm not leaving.*"

A ghost of a smile flickered across Savvy's tense lips at Sky's stubborn tone.

"You can stay for now," replied the doctor, but her voice, too, held a serious, no-nonsense tone. "You're going to have to prepare yourself for a long wait. As soon as I get the test results and finish my examination I'm almost certain Ms. Alexander will be going up to surgery. It looks like appendicitis. I think the appendix may have already ruptured."

Within half an hour the decision was made—surgery. In a twilight fog Savvy felt competent hands slide her throbbing body onto the operating table. Glaring overhead lights made her eyes squeeze shut. Then everything went blessedly black and painfree after the anesthesiologist injected a large needle into a vein in Savvy's restrained arm.

When Savvy opened her eyes again she felt groggy and squinted into the cool shadows of a strange hospital room. The uncurtained window across the way revealed the gray light of dawn. She wiggled her toes and fingers and knew she was still in one piece. Amazing! she mused. She had thought the pain of the evening before would surely blow her apart. When she tried to speak, the only sound that slipped between her dry lips was a low moan. Instantly Sky was at her side.

"Savvy? Honey, it's all over. You're going to be just fine." His voice sounded gravelly as if he had been sleeping. He picked up her slim hand and tenderly kissed the fingertips. "Thank God we got here in time. The appendix was just about to burst." This time his voice broke with suppressed emotion, and Savvy thought she saw a tear glisten on his stubbly cheek. "Are you in much pain?"

She tried to smile but her mouth refused to listen to her command. She was still feeling the aftereffects of the anesthetic. "I'm a little achey," she managed to whisper. "And I'm so-o-o sleepy."

Sky leaned forward and kissed her forehead. "It's okay, honey. You just sleep. Rest is what you need."

Suddenly she remembered the scene that had precipitated her attack. She clutched at Sky's shirt, trying to hold on, but her fingers had no strength. "Don't leave me, Sky," she cried hysterically. "I don't want to be alone."

"Honey, honey. I won't leave you. I'll stay right here until you wake up again."

"Promise?"

Her one-word plea made Sky smile almost paternally. She sounded like a sweet child of ten. Lying in the large white bed, she looked like a child, too, he thought. When people got sick they always looked smaller, he decided, refusing to think how he must look after spending the night's vigil in a straight-backed chair in the corner. "I promise, baby. Now go to sleep."

While she slept Savvy knew in a dim sort of way that nurses checked on her. Her pulse was taken, her heartbeat recorded, and the I.V. dripping into her arm was adjusted periodically. It was noon before she awakened fully, and the first person she saw was Sky. He was seated next to her bed, holding her hand. The I.V. had been removed.

"You don't look bad for having spent the night in a chair," she murmured softly.

His face lit up at her observation. "Not to mention the wear and tear on my heart. Damn, woman, you scared me to death." His truthful words were cushioned by his wide white smile. "And you should have seen me two hours ago. I looked like a bum, but I borrowed your shower and Hooker ran over with a change of clothes and my razor."

"You look good enough to eat." She grinned drunkenly.

He raised his brow wickedly and gave her a patronizing wink. "That's a good sign. The patient's hungry."

Savvy groaned loudly. "If you're talking about *real* food, forget it! I still feel turned inside out." She tried to move to a more comfortable position in her bed and winced with pain.

Immediately Sky became jangled. "Wait! I don't know if you're supposed to move yet. Let me get the nurse." Without waiting for a response he turned and ran out the door. Savvy could hear his voice ringing down the hallway. "Nurse! Nurse, Ms. Alexander needs you." When he returned a moment later with a flustered nurse in tow, Savvy's red face showed plainly how she felt about Sky's high-handedness.

"What seems to be the trouble, Ms. Alexander?" queried the breathless nurse. "Are you in pain?"

Savvy shook her head. "I'm feeling quite well really. It wasn't my idea to call you. I was just wondering if I could change positions. I'm sorry if you were disturbed unnecessarily, Nurse Collins," she apologized, reading the name on the nurse's badge.

"I'm glad to see you're awake," the nurse said. "Of course you can move. In fact, after I check you out, we're going to take a little stroll around your room." She turned to Sky and gave him a nurse's typical commanding look, which was met by his own stubborn-jawed glare. "You've got five minutes, Detective Brady, then out you go. We've got work to do and then our patient is going to have some lunch before she rests again. *Five minutes*," she cautioned once more as she left the room.

Sky's black look revealed how unaccustomed he was to taking orders. "Who the hell does she think she is?"

Savvy couldn't contain a little chuckle. "This is *her* turf, Sky. I'm afraid she's the boss here."

His dark look disappeared and he smiled beguilingly. "She won't keep me away for long, Savvy. I'll be back this evening." He bent over and carefully kissed her warm, relaxed mouth. "Thank God you're okay. I'll see you in a little while."

"I love you, Sky. Thanks for getting me here in time."

He kissed her again and sighed from the depth of his being. "Same here, honey. I'll see you later."

It was evening when she awoke from another long nap. She turned carefully onto her side and mentally checked her discomfort. With a happy smile and a long sigh of relief she realized she felt quite wonderful. Glancing around her she spotted a large vase of a dozen long-stemmed red roses on the dresser. The room was filled with their heady fragrance. Each breath she took seemed to assure her that she would soon be back in Sky's warm embrace. The doctor had come in earlier and told her everything had gone smoothly and, if there were no complications, Savvy would be going home in two days.

"We don't make much fuss over an appendectomy anymore," Dr. Lord had told her. "Now, heart transplants we keep longer," she teased.

After the doctor checked her over and left, Savvy asked one of the Gray Lady volunteers if she could purchase a brush and some makeup. Sky had left her ten dollars to pay for the items. Later, as she tried to repair the ravages of the terrifying night, Savvy recalled the doctor's last words. Lucky for her, she mused, she wouldn't be needing a heart operation. Sky would be back shortly.

When he arrived during visiting hours he seemed refreshed and grinned happily as he leaned over to kiss her hello. "Hey, you're looking chipper, honey. All soft and rosy. Got a heavy date?"

"Just with the only man I've ever wanted to marry . . . and he's just about perfect," she teased, returning his kiss.

Sucking in his breath, he glanced furtively over his shoulder. "Do you think the Wicked Witch would mind if I crawled in with you?"

"Probably," Savvy answered softly, surprised at the rise in her temperature over one gentle kiss. "You'll just have to wait two days until I get back home again."

"Two days!" he exclaimed. "They can't release you so soon. You've just had an operation." His dark scowl returned in full force. "I thought this place was staffed with competent people. That can't be right, Savvy."

She giggled at Sky's seeming inability to grasp the minor aspects of her surgery. "Sure, they know what they're doing. It was a very simple procedure. Nothing to worry about. Everything's fine now and I can go home day after tomorrow."

"It still seems too soon." He grumbled petulantly. "I'll hire a nurse to stay with you full-time." Snapping his fingers, he added, "Better yet, you'll come home with me and I'll nurse you back to glowing health." The lecherous sparkle in his teal blue eyes caused Savvy to laugh out loud. Instantly she held her stomach.

"How can you think of sex when I'm lying in a bed of pain?"

"Ver-y eas-i-ly!" He growled, smoothing his large hands across her shoulders and over her firm breasts. He watched as his fingers teased circles around her nipples until they were hard, rounded bubbles beneath the sheet. "See?"

"That's exactly what I'm talking about!" But her breathless words fell far short of her intended serious tone. Clearing her throat she continued. "I'm going back to my apartment. Teri will look after me for a day or two. I'm almost well already. It's no big deal, honestly."

"I like my idea better," he argued stubbornly. Savvy thought he looked like a little boy who'd just been told he couldn't have a cookie.

"I'll be there soon, darling," she promised as they kissed good night. The gong had already signaled the end of visiting hours.

• • •

Even for a day in the hospital, Savvy decided the time sped by on Saturday. She had her meals to eat, a shower to take, and Sky popped in every chance he got. He sent more flowers and brought stacks of magazines that she knew she'd never find time to read with everything else that was required of a patient on the mend.

When Sky arrived for the last visit of the evening, Savvy had good news. "The doctor was in to see me. She's discharging me in the morning. Isn't that great?" She expected to hear a joyous response to her announcement. Instead Sky stood stiff-legged and silent, gazing out the window. His tension seemed to fill the entire room. "Did you hear me, Sky?" she asked gently.

He didn't turn and his grim answer chilled her blood. "Yes, I heard you. I was just thinking."

The fear she had experienced the night of her attack returned in full force. "What are you thinking about?" She didn't know if she wanted to hear his reply.

"I could have lost you, Savvy. You could have been taken from me in the blink of an eye."

"From a simple appendectomy?" She gasped in disbelief. Trying to lighten the mood, she teased him. "You're not going to get rid of me so easily."

Sky turned abruptly and walked to the side of her bed. His eyes were sad, devoid of their usual sparkle, his face pale and forlorn. "Stranger things have happened, honey."

Savvy's heart almost stopped at the look on his face and she tried to gather him in her arms. "Nothing's happened, Sky. I'm going to be fine. Please believe me."

"I figure I've been pushing my luck," he said softly. "Maybe I'm asking for too much."

Fear became a sharp knife in her heart. "But I'm here, Sky. There wasn't a million-to-one chance that anything was going to go wrong."

"With my luck, I could have experienced that long shot, Savvy." He shuddered beneath her touch. "God, I've never been so scared."

"I know," she said soothingly. "I would have felt the same way." Desperately she tried to get him to look on the bright side. "I'm going home tomorrow morning. And very soon I'll be able to show you just how healthy I am." Purposely she put a flirting lilt in her voice.

He shook his head, trying to dispel his dark mood. Conjuring a plastic smile, he gazed down at her. She was still pale and fragile looking. Would he ever get over the fear of losing her? he wondered. Would he ever be at peace? "I'll hold you to it, slugger." He caressed her soft breasts and kissed her. "Seems to me we have some unfinished business."

His echoing words brought tears to Savvy's eyes. She clung to him a moment longer, whispering sweet words of love into his ear. "I hope we never finish, darling. I love you so much. More than you'll ever know."

"Me, too, honey. I'll see you in the morning." He kissed her good night and turned toward the door. His hand formed a fist against the wooden barrier. His body stiffened and grew still. Sighing heavily, he bid her good-bye. "So long, honey." And he was gone.

After Sky left, Savvy had difficulty falling asleep.

She finally accepted a mild sedative. Rest was what she needed, she told herself, pushing aside her troubling thoughts. She was going to have a big day tomorrow. She was going home.

Sky didn't come to pick her up on Sunday morning. Instead he sent Hooker. When she heard the door open and turned around with a radiant smile on her lips, there he was.

"Hi, patient. Ready to go home?" Hooker seemed to be overenthusiastic in his greeting.

"Where's Sky?" A frown creased Savvy's forehead. "He promised he would come."

"He got called into the station," Hooker explained. "Something about closing the case on Jocko, I think."

"I wish he would have called me. I was counting on him." She was suddenly aware of how her words might hurt Hooker's feelings and hastened to make amends. "Not that I'm not happy to see you. After all, I don't think the Stallion Man would do this kind of favor for just anyone." She matched his grin and gathered the last of her meager possessions. "I'm sure glad Teri brought over my clothes yesterday afternoon. I'd look pretty silly walking out of here in a hospital gown."

Hooker winked and gave her a quick, seductive perusal. "Me thinks you'd look damned sexy, Savena, darlin'!" When her face had blushed crimson, he grinned. "And you know what else?" he added. "I met your friend Teri the other day. She's damned sexy too." When Savvy laughed, he was satisfied. That very friend was waiting for them when they arrived at

Savvy's apartment. Teri carefully hugged Savvy. "Welcome home," she said.

Savvy glanced around her apartment, looking at the furnishings with interest. "Everything looks strange, yet familiar. It's so good to be home." She slid onto her comfortable sofa and sighed. "Yes, it's really great to be back."

Teri excused herself and went into the kitchen to brew some of her famous herb tea. "Guaranteed to perk you up in no time at all," she promised.

When Hooker saw that Savvy would be well taken care of, he got up to leave. "I've got a booking in an hour, Savvy. I'm sorry I have to run, but fame calls." He winked and kissed her on the cheek. "Take care of yourself now. Sky said he'd be by this evening to see you."

She patted his cheek and smiled sleepily. "I think I'd better take a long nap then. Thank you for bringing me home, Hooker. You're a good friend."

"That's what all the girls say!" He called good-bye to Teri and sauntered out the door.

"I could use a friend like that," exclaimed Teri when she returned with Savvy's hot tea. "What a man!"

"Who knows? He might be the one for you."

"Dreamer!" Teri scoffed. "Drink your tea while it's hot, then it's off to beddie-bye with you, cookie. You're not over this yet."

"No, I'm not." But her agreeable words went much deeper. Somehow Savvy knew Sky was experiencing troubled thoughts again.

That evening, when Sky had not arrived by nine o'clock, Teri suggested Savvy call his home. Hooker answered.

"You mean he didn't call you?" When she confirmed his outraged question, he told her everything he knew. "Sky's left town."

"*What?*"

"Yeah, darlin'. He packed a bag and took off this afternoon. Said he had some thinking to do. But the damn fool promised he'd call you first. I could kick him for doing this to you. Do you know what it's all about?"

Savvy held one hand over her middle and the other over her aching heart. The phone remained cradled to her ear, nestled by her shoulder. "I'm not sure, Hooker," she whispered, "but I think it has something to do with his belief that his luck isn't going to hold out."

"*Damn!*" Hooker's voice exploded over the line. "I thought he was over that."

"Apparently he isn't. Look, I won't keep you. You're probably busy. Will you call me when he gets back?"

"I give you my solemn promise. But I'm not sure he'll be able to talk to you."

"Why?"

"He's going to have some trouble speaking with his front teeth knocked out!" Hooker growled angrily.

"Oh, Hooker! What would I do without you?"

"I'll never give you a chance to find out, sweet darlin'. Now get some rest and try not to worry. Sky will be back in a few days, I'm certain."

"I wish I could be so sure. Good night, Hooker. And thanks again." When she hung up the phone she began to cry softly. "I'm losing him, Teri. And I don't know what I can do about it. I can't keep fighting ghosts."

Gathering Savvy in her arms, Teri rocked her gently. "You're going to get a good night's sleep and things will look brighter in the morning."

"Have I ever told you what a cock-eyed optimist you are?" Slowly she stood and walked into her bedroom.

"Does that mean I should have my eyes examined?" Teri put a crazy cross-eyed expression on her beautiful Nordic face.

Savvy couldn't help laughing. "Or your head!"

Three nights passed before Savvy got Hooker's frantic call. It was after midnight. "Savvy, do you feel well enough to come over here?"

Instantly Savvy was wide awake. She had dozed in front of the television set watching a late-night movie. Teri had gone home and she was alone and lonely. "What is it, Hooker? Is Sky back home? Has something happened to him?" Listening to his grumbling she shouted, "*Hooker!* Is Sky there?"

"His worthless body is here, all right, but I don't know where the hell his mind is," he barked, but he sounded worried too. "He came home about three hours ago and said he wanted to talk to me. I thought I could be of some help so I settled down to listen. But he also wanted to drink. He began to hit the booze that I'd ordered for the engagement party. I honestly don't think he's going to stop until he finishes it. I switched to ginger ale after the first three, but he's really tying one on, Savvy. It's not like him. He's never tried to drown his troubles in a bottle. And he keeps talking like some recorded message."

"What's he saying?" Her heart was pounding in her chest like a bass drum.

"He says he hasn't got the courage to test his luck. He keeps muttering about watching over you, keeping you safe from killers and kidnappers when a simple thing like an appendectomy could snatch you out of his arms. I tried to assure him that you were doing just great, but he cut me off and added to his list. He shouted that you could die in childbirth or even be killed crossing the street."

Suddenly there was a loud crash in the background. "Dammit, Brady! I told you to stay put," Hooker hollered.

Speaking to Savvy again, he apologized. "Sorry I yelled into the phone, darlin'. I've got a problem here. Old son is getting *drunk as a skunk!*"

Savvy could picture Hooker scowling at Sky's staggering form. Her composure broke and she began to cry softly. "I give up, Hooker," she whispered brokenly. "When he gets really pickled, stuff his head into a jar and we'll take it to a lab for expert analysis."

"He doesn't need experts, darlin'. All he needs is you." Hooker's sensual voice rippled up and down Savvy's spine. Unaccountably she wondered if falling in love with the beautiful Stallion Man would have been any easier than her tempestuous adventure with his sexy sidekick. Of course she knew the answer even before she finished exploring the idea. Both men were complex creatures.

"He has me, Hooker . . . if he wants me." She sniffled against the cradled receiver.

"Listen to me, Savvy," Hooker pleaded. "There's a dark side of him that's afraid he's going to lose you, just when he needs and wants you most. He's lost so many times before. His mother when he was very young and just becoming a man; then his grandfather, and finally his father. That 'Dear John' letter was hard on him and came right before the attack on our patrol. Everyone was lost in that ambush, Savvy. The only ones left were Sky and me. Even that fiasco with a woman he never loved hurt him. Don't you see, Savvy?" he whispered, feeling as if he were sharing information he had sworn on his life to protect. "It's his *secret inner fear.*"

"I can't do any more, Hooker." Suddenly she felt completely drained of energy. "He's going to have to battle this demon alone."

Hooker had to make one last attempt to convince her, even if it meant laying a guilt trip on her. "Look, he saved my life. And remember that he helped you fight your secret fear, lady. Maybe, just maybe, you're going to have to save him now."

"You really know how to kick a girl when she's down, Mr. Jablonski!" Tears continued to stream down her pale cheeks.

"You're the only one who can help him through this tough time, Savvy. I won't apologize for my methods if it makes you think. I love that guy."

"I will think about it," she promised softly. "Take care of him for me, Hooker. I love him too." Gently she replaced the receiver and sank down onto the floor, crying as if her heart had broken into a million pieces.

Ten

If anyone could have watched Savvy that night, they would have thought she was having a nervous breakdown. Wandering around the house she began cleaning, using every ounce of strength in her tormented and still weak body.

She sat on a chair in the bathtub and cleaned the ceramic tile with a toothbrush. She tried to scrub the floor, but couldn't stay on her hands and knees long enough. Instead she waxed every stick of furniture until each piece sparkled like a polish commercial. Breathing raggedly and sweating profusely, she changed her bedding but was unable to take it downstairs to the laundry room by the pool. As the sun was peeking over the treetops, she was wiping haphazardly at her bedroom windowpane. Distracted by a plant that needed to be trimmed, she stopped halfway through and tended to the greenery.

Work was what she was trying to do, weak though she was. Work was something she had learned to do at her mother's knee. Whenever times were troubled, Mama started scrubbing. She claimed she could think better. But for all the energy Savvy had expended, she knew she wasn't one step closer to a solution to *her* troubles. When the phone rang at eight she dragged her sleep-starved body over and answered with a lost child's voice.

"What's wrong?" It was Teri with her uncanny radar for knowing when she was needed.

"My world's just crashed down around my ears," Savvy answered, beginning to howl like a banshee. "I don't know what to do."

"I'll be right there." The phone went dead and almost before Savvy could hang up the receiver, Teri was pounding up her stairs and knocking to be let inside. When Savvy opened the door Teri was redfaced from running full out, but she pulled her friend into her arms and let her cry until she could cry no more. "Now, tell me."

Brokenly Savvy explained the horrendous situation. "He's afraid he's going to lose me," she lamented, blowing her nose into another offered tissue. "In some perverse way he's pushing me out of his life . . . because he can't take the risk."

Teri fixed them both a cup of herb tea while she continued to ponder the problem. "That old cliché about no one knowing what tomorrow is going to bring won't help much in this case, I don't think. Sky has had more than his share of heartbreak. It's almost as if he's expecting to be disappointed again." She gave Savvy a narrowed questioning look. "You still love him, don't you?"

"More than I ever thought I could love any man," Savvy replied, wringing her hands together. "I just don't know what to do."

When Teri saw that her friend's face was beginning to cloud up into another anguished crying fit, she tried a little shock treatment. "Well, you damn well better think of something, girl. He's the man for you, and *you know it!*"

Teri's scolding tone brought Savvy's drooping head and shoulders to attention. "Lord, don't you start trying to make me feel like it's my fault too," she retorted, beginning to bristle at her friend's strident voice.

Teri smiled secretly and noted with pleasure the return of some color to Savvy's cheeks. "*I'd* sure fight to keep him. What have you been telling me all these weeks about him? He never ever has taken you for granted. That's something that's always bugged the hell out of you in your other relationships."

"There were *so many!*" Savvy said sarcastically, trying to pull Teri off the subject for a while.

"There were a few," she countered knowingly. "And I don't think you can accuse him of being possessive either. That also drives you up the wall, right?"

"Right," Savvy agreed quietly, feeling her mind begin to operate in something like its normal process again. "I've got to have room to be me."

"All right," Teri continued, sounding more like a lawyer than Savvy sometimes did. "We're agreed that he doesn't take you for granted. We're also agreed that he's not the jealous type." She walked back and forth across the living-room carpet, tapping her chin with her forefinger, pondering the evidence. "What we have here is a man who loves you to distraction, and who is afraid that *Fate* will take you away from him. I'd suggest that you give him a great big dose of love. That should convince the little dickens." She chuckled happily. "You've got to prove to him that the Black Brady curse is broken."

"But how?"

"You can court him, Savvy."

"What?" She had to laugh in spite of the seriousness of Teri's proposal.

"Hey! It's a new world. No woman has to sit at home waiting for the phone to ring. Use some of your natural aggressive spirit and go after him."

"Do you think it could work?" A sketchy plan was beginning to take shape in her spinning brain.

"What have you got to lose . . . except the man you love?" Teri could tell by the lively sparks in Savvy's eyes that she was coming back into the land of the living. "*Go for it!*" Teri said. "And don't take no for an answer." She gave Savvy another hug and a smack on her seat before she said good-bye. "You can do it, girl. I know it." Then she closed the door quietly behind her, leaving Savvy lost in a swirling selection of possibilities.

Grabbing a pad of paper and a pen, Savvy dropped down into the middle of her huge bed and sat cross-legged, thinking. Eventually she began to outline her plan of attack. She was fighting for her man, she told herself bravely. This was war! But a war in which both parties would be the ultimate victors. Writing feverishly, she worked hard, then fell asleep until late afternoon. The written plan was propped against the other pillow as if it were a billboard announcing the return of Sky Brady's lean, strong body to her side.

When Savvy awoke she raided the refrigerator, suddenly famished because she hadn't eaten since the night before. Girding herself for the good fight, she showered and washed her hair. The hot stream of hard spray revitalized her and she felt ready. Tomorrow morning she would begin her battle for Sky's heart. She had decided to give her plan seven days for success. Devoutly she prayed that it wouldn't take an entire week; already she missed Sky so much. But she would give it one week . . . seven days.

And what if it doesn't work? prodded her own vulnerable heart. Her cry of protest caught in her throat at the possibility of failure. "*No!* No, no, no, no," she exclaimed. "I won't even think about failing. Not now."

The first package arrived bright and early Friday at the Brady residence. Hooker answered the door and tipped the delivery boy. Recognizing the bright balloon paper as Savvy's company trademark, he sauntered out to the back and dropped the box into Sky's unsuspecting lap. Sky's swift movement to catch the bundle brought a loud protesting groan of pain. Even the dark glasses and hours in the hot sun the day before hadn't baked out his monumental hangover. "Dammit, Hooker! You know I'm dying."

Hooker laughed loud and long, further irritating his friend. "I thought you'd want this surprise package as soon as possible," he said, still chuckling. "Looks like it's from your new business partner." Without another word he spun around on his heel and went back into the kitchen, where he was preparing one of his gourmet lunches.

Sky warily eyed the brightly wrapped box. He barely had the strength to tear off the paper, then he jumped back in surprise—further irritating his throbbing skull—when a bright multicolored balloon popped up and floated from its tether. A ribbon of gold held a note and a police whistle. He touched the whistle and decided it was the same one he had given to her for safety when she ran in the early morning. He had to squint his eyes and read very, very slowly. "Next time you go on a toot, use this instead. It could save your fat head!"

Hooker couldn't suppress his curiosity and ambled back onto the patio to see what the box contained. Leaning over, he read the note and then put the whistle in his mouth, splitting the air with an ear-deafening squeal. "Cute idea," he said, immediately returning to his kitchen because Sky was holding his head in trembling hands, trying to protect his brain from total annihilation. Once inside, Hooker howled like a demented soul for a full minute, furtively glancing over his shoulder to see if Sky was coming after him. So much for quiet tranquility, he decided, still laughing to himself. Then he took pity on his friend and made him a Bloody Mary. But his step had lightened when he returned with his peace offering. Savvy had begun to fight!

Saturday brought the second present. Not willing to undergo another blinding, explosive contribution by Hooker, Sky carried the box to his room and locked the door behind him. Sitting on the edge of his bed he pulled off the wrapping. This time a red ball floated out. Another note and a thick piece of unmarked paper danced from the string. The note read, "Paste this on your forehead, genius!"

Warily he stumbled into the bathroom and flipped on the light. After three days, he still had a headache. Why, he asked himself. The answer was obvious— Savvy! Standing in front of the mirror he laid the plain thick paper in his palm. Almost at once writing revealed itself, but he couldn't read it. Disgruntled he realized it was reverse printing and he lifted the fast-disappearing message—now that he had taken it from his hand—to his warm forehead. Leaning forward he read: "I'm the only one in the world who can cure your fever. Savvy."

Knowing there was truth in the statement, but disconcerted that she had the nerve to say it, he jammed the items back into the box and folded down the lid. He spent the rest of the day swimming and thinking. And refusing to answer Hooker's teasing questions about the box's contents.

Sunday's balloon was brilliant yellow. Dangling from the string was a small magnifying glass. "It's elementary, my dear Sky-lar. The clue? I love you," Savvy's message read. On Monday, Sky was really getting jumpy, wondering what was coming next. He found he was half mad and half anticipating each day's surprise. A green balloon jumped out at him. Hanging beneath the bobbing ball was a tiny set of semaphore flags. The accompanying note read, "The message is clear. I need you."

Sky couldn't suppress a little grin. She was one competitive woman, he thought, feeling a glimmer of respect at her brave determination. Then his dark side wiped the smile from his lips. "She'll get tired of her little game soon enough." But of course Savvy had made a commitment . . . and she wasn't a *quitter*!

That evening Savvy worked in her home office preparing Tuesday's offering. This time she used a much larger box to hold her serpentine surprise. She had filled over a dozen long snake balloons of various colors, twisting and bending them into a contorted jumble. She anchored the bizarre knot to a purple balloon along with her note. "I hope this message sends him flying back," she said aloud, rereading her heartfelt words, knowing they were nothing less than the truth.

Hooker discovered Sky hugging the knotted slim tubes in his arms the next morning. Silently he took the note from his friend's stiff fingers and read. "I'm all tied into knots because I want you." Shaking his head sadly, he glanced at Sky and saw the look of distress on his tanned face. "You're weakening, old son," he observed. "Why don't you put both your hearts back together again?"

Sky shook his head sadly. Lost was what he was, thought Hooker. Taking one last stab at the problem, he said, "Dammit, man, she loves you. And you love her. Go to her." Not getting the response he wished for, he threw up his hands in disgust and went back into the kitchen to relieve his emotions in a tussle with a loaf of rye bread. Pounding and kneading the dough, he thought he had never met such a stubborn, stupid soul as Skylar Brady!

Unknown to the sad separated couple Teri and Hooker had been trying to keep tabs on the developing scenario. While Hooker was cajoling and prodding in the Brady house, Teri was continuing her stouthearted encouragement of Savvy not to give up. By Tuesday evening, when Savvy was preparing the sixth box, Teri could see that her friend was about to throw in the towel in defeat. "You can't give up," she pleaded, holding the blue balloon while Savvy fastened a colorful sad-faced clown doll to the tether. She was crying while she printed out the companion message. It was a sorrowful lament of her breaking heart. Teri read it as she tied it around the neck of the little doll. "It's no fun clowning around without my Superman." Teri had to swallow hard to keep from joining Savvy in a few distressing tears.

Patting Savvy's rounded shoulder, she tried heroically to restore some measure of Savvy's fighting spirit. "You gave it seven days, Savvy. And that leaves one more shot left, right?"

Savvy nodded dejectedly.

"What are you going to do for the finale?"

"I'm going for broke on the last one." She laughed sadly.

"You're saving the big guns till last, huh?"

"Something like that." Finishing the wrapping Savvy put the package by the front door for the seven o'clock pickup in the morning. "What are you going to do tomorrow night, Teri?" Savvy herself had gone nowhere all week and was feeling cut off from the rest of the world. "Would you like to go to a movie?"

Teri blushed and laughed nervously. "You're never going to believe this, Savvy, but Hooker has asked me to dinner and dancing."

"And why wouldn't I believe it?" Savvy said. "You're a beautiful woman, worthy of any man," she added staunchly.

"But the *Stallion Man*!" Teri exclaimed, rolling her eyes to the ceiling in an uninhibited swoon.

"He's a good man," Savvy replied, smiling at Teri's response. "Don't believe all the P.R. hype. He's a rock when he needs to be, believe me."

"You can join us if you'd like," Teri said eagerly. "I'm sure Hooker wouldn't mind."

Savvy laughed. "Oh, wouldn't he just! Anyway I've got one more day of battle . . . and I think I'd better hang around." Hugging Teri as she walked her to the door, Savvy waxed philosophic again. "You know, I never fully understood the meaning of the phrase 'prisoner of love.' Now I think I understand. It's a very lonely existence."

"I'll call you in the morning, okay? We'll go for a walk and that'll make you feel better."

Savvy agreed, but knew she'd never feel better again . . . not unless Sky came back to her.

Down the road Sky sat in his study, staring at an old rerun of *Happy Days*. He nursed a warm beer and lit up another cigarette—it finished the second pack of the day. His mouth felt dry and rough. Even the beer couldn't wash away the stale taste of too many cigarettes. When Hooker looked in on him before he left for the evening, he sniffed disdainfully at the overpowering stench of burning tobacco and threw open the French doors to let some fresh air into the room.

"My God, Brady, this place smells like a cheap saloon." He waved his arms around his body, lamenting the odor that was permeating his dashing black outfit.

"So who's asking you to stay?" Sky grumbled. "And this is imported beer . . . it *isn't cheap*, Jablonski!"

"You're a real sunbeam tonight," Hooker shot back. All week long he'd tried to reason with his friend, tried to convince him that he was making the biggest mistake of his life. He'd even called in Jake Connelly as his able assistant to argue the case, but Sky had been adamant. "Dammit, Brady. When in the hell are you going to go see Savvy? You're never going to be happy again unless you do."

Sullenly Sky drained his warm beer and ground out his cigarette in an ashtray filled to overflowing. "I'll talk to her when I get good and ready, Hooker. I may *never* be ready . . . so get off my back!"

Hooker had never seen Sky in such a state of mental turmoil. Not even after the firefight overseas. He'd tried everything he could think of to convince Sky to change his mind. There wasn't anything else he could do so he shrugged and quietly bid Sky good night. "I won't be too late, buddy. Oh, and incidentally, tomorrow evening I'm taking Teri Pegasus out for dinner and a few dances."

Life came back into Sky's eyes at the mention of Savvy's best friend. "See if you can find out how Savvy is, will you?"

Hooker snorted and peeled off a string of expletives

that would have curled most men's hair. But it didn't even raise Sky's eyebrows. "If you want to know if she's been as miserable as you this week, the answer is *yes!*" After calling him a damn fool intent on ruining the lives of two of his best friends, Hooker refused to answer any more of Sky's cutting remarks. He left, leaving rubber in the driveway when he pulled away.

Sky spent the rest of the night in his bedroom, pondering one floating balloon after another, each with its message and symbol of Savvy's love. He missed her so much he felt like he was bleeding inside.

The next morning, when he received his sixth box, he tore it open, somehow hoping she could force his self-admitted obstinate decision to stay away from her. When the sad-faced clown came floating out of the package, he smiled in spite of himself. Her pointed words reminded him of their first meeting when Savvy had been the saddest clown in town and he had rescued her, becoming her personal Superman. His loins ached with his need for her. How could Fate be so cruel as to thrust him into a situation where, instead of being in firm control, he had lost his heart? He cursed angrily. "Love isn't for me, dammit," he yelled. "I'm jinxed! I'll only make Savvy's life miserable."

Unable to stay in the house a minute longer, he jammed the balloon back into its box and closed the lid. Tossing it into a corner of the entry hall he pulled his keys from his pocket and ran to his car. The torment of his soul showed in the deepening creases in his face. He had aged ten years during this week of hell. Starting the engine, he pulled out of the drive and headed north to the country.

Subconsciously he must have known where he was going. However, he was genuinely surprised when he stopped the car along the quiet country lane at the edge of his property. Shaken and still upset, he climbed from his silver sports car and walked blindly toward the crest of the nearest hill, coming to a halt inside the gate of the family cemetery. Tears misted his vision as he looked from one weathered tombstone to the next. To the right were the markers for Pappy and his wife, whom Sky had never known. In the center were the graves of his parents, Clara and Benjamin Brady. Far back on the left were the stones marking his great-grandparents' resting places. When his time came Sky knew that he, too, would be laid to rest in this plot. Somehow it was a comforting thought. Yet a hollow feeling filled him where his heart should have been. He imagined the inscription on his stone: Here lies Skylar Brady. He knew love but was never allowed to keep it for long.

Sinking to his knees he sobbed openly for the first time in his adult life. He cried for all that he'd lost. He cried for all that might have been. Wrapped inside his misery he didn't hear the quiet footsteps of his old friend Mr. Jablonski, Hooker's father. The man gently touched Sky's convulsing shoulders, letting him know that he was there.

Quickly Sky choked back his tears and furtively wiped his shirt sleeve across his flushed face. "Hi, Pop." He coughed hoarsely to cover his embarrassment and sadness. "What brings you up here?"

"I figured I might find you here, Sky. Hooker called

a while ago asking me to be on the lookout for you when he saw you take off north," he explained. "This is where you always come when you've got nowhere else to go."

Sky nodded and rose to his feet to face the man. "I'm okay now, Pop. Just a little problem I had to face."

Mr. Jablonski squinted his eyes against the sun and seemed to look right through Sky. "You haven't faced it, son. Don't you think it's time you did?" He grasped Sky's muscled shoulders with an iron grip. "Go to her, boy. One minute with the woman you love is worth all the risk in the world. Don't you see that?"

"It's damn hard to keep trying, Pop," he said, wanting to do as his friend suggested more than anything else. "I just don't think I can take another disappointment. It hurts too much."

"Hogwash!" Sky jerked his head up in surprise. It was the closest thing to swearing that he'd ever heard cross Mr. Jablonski's lips. "You're hurtin' *now*, aren't you? Go to her." Locking his penetrating gaze with Sky's he asked one last question. "You do love her, don't ya?"

A bittersweet smile curved Sky's mouth. "More than I can tell you, Pop."

Gathering him into a great bear hug of encouragement, Mr. Jablonski said again, "Then go to her, son. *Go to her.*"

Driving back to his city house, Sky heard birds singing and enjoyed the warm sunshine as it beat down on his open car. Laughing in relief, as if the weight of the world had been lifted from his shoulders, he viewed his life in a new light. He was going to see Savvy. He'd made up his mind. But by the time he pulled into his driveway his exuberant smile had disappeared. "What if she's gotten tired of waiting?" he asked himself. "I've got to have a plan to convince her that we're going to make it . . . *together*!" He spent the rest of the day mapping his strategy.

Eleven

Wednesday was the longest day of Savvy's life. She had hoped against hope that Sky would come to her after being reminded of their first meeting. Instead the phone hung silent on the wall. She was not even given the opportunity to raise her spirits with a false alarm. All business calls were now being handled at a new number. Despondently she prowled around her apartment. There wasn't one item left to clean and polish. Her mother would be proud of her, she thought in dismay.

The news program on television that could usually interest her held no fascination today. Trade publications that she should have been reading were tossed carelessly to the floor when she bolted from her couch and began prowling again. With nothing left to do she wrapped the last of her seven packages for Sky. Sitting in the middle of her bed she berated herself for doing a poor job of it. This was her last chance. It had to be prepared to the best of her ability. Angrily she began again and forced herself to concentrate until it was completed. Then she set the box on the floor next to her dresser, ready for the special Thursday morning pickup she had arranged.

Toward evening she walked to the phone at least a dozen times to call Sky, to plead with him to come back. Four times she grabbed her purse and van keys to drive to his house. She would hesitate at the door and then draw back. The final time she was actually sitting in Violet, the motor revved up and ready to go, but she knew she couldn't go to him. Unless Sky came to grips with his fateful demons she didn't have a chance. Yes, she'd tried to help him the best way she knew how. As Teri had confirmed, the man was worth fighting for, but how did one fight illusionary fears? "Oh God," she prayed, "please, please bring him back to me."

When evening came Sky was prepared for their meeting. He carefully crammed all his ballooned messages into his car and drove slowly to her apartment complex. He fervently prayed that she would give him a chance to make this week of misery up to her.

Savvy was sitting on her sofa, trying to read. Her sensory equipment snapped to attention when she heard the familiar sound of Sky's automobile engine. When she heard the car door slam she leaped up from the couch and pressed her face against the glass of her patio door, straining to catch a glimpse of his beloved body. All she could see was a bunch of rainbow-colored balloons bobbing along the sidewalk. She tried to still her nervous fingers as they smoothed her champagne curls away from her flushed face. A tremulous smile appeared then darted away as she worked to control her excited features. Sky was coming!

Transfixed, she stood in the center of the living room, listening to his slow, measured footfall on the stairs outside. She nearly jumped out of her skin when she heard a hesitant knock at her door. Then she was flying across the room, flinging the door wide to welcome him. What met her eyes, however, was nothing like she'd ever imagined. In Sky's place was the saddest-looking clown Savvy had ever seen. "Sky? Sky, is that you?"

The figure nodded in a slow, tormented movement and shuffled into the living room. He looked at her with eyes that rivaled those of a champion bloodhound. An appropriate comparison, her spinning brain interjected. It didn't look as if he could find words to express his sadness and loneliness. He would not speak. He only stood there in his clown makeup: Pale red nose, white outlined lips shaped into a downcast, dejected expression, woebegone sloping black brows, and blue diamond shapes painted across his lids, punctuated by a single glistening teardrop drawn on his darkened cheek. Her heart was breaking just to look at his sorrowful expression.

What should she do? she wondered frantically. Should she ask him to explain? Oh, dear heaven, tell me what to do, she begged. As if on a silent signal, the answer came. She gazed into Sky's sad eyes and whispered, "Is there something you wanted to say?"

At once he began to nod so hard she feared he would hurt his neck. A tiny smile tugged at her trembling lips as she noted that his companions—the balloons—were bobbing right along with him. "Do continue, Sad Clown. You have my undivided attention," she encouraged, closing the door behind him.

Miming his way through a clearly planned program, he made himself understood and Savvy interpreted. Grabbing at his chest he showed her how sad he was feeling. He put his two curved hands side by side and broke an imaginary object, then pointed to his heart.

"You are very, very sad. Your heart is breaking."

He rubbed his tattered lapel to emphasize her words. He then mimed a pointed hat atop his battered cap.

"Are you saying you're a dunce? A fool?"

Again his head bobbed his agreement, making his face one of the chorus at his side.

"Maybe we've both been foolish?" she ventured tremulously. In answer, he shrugged and raised his sad brows. Then he put his ragged gloved hands together in a prayerful gesture and knelt before her. "You don't need forgiveness, my darling," she murmured. "All you need is my love as I need yours. That's all we'll ever need, Sky."

Slowly he rose to his feet, a whimsical smile fighting to overcome his downcast painted features. His eyes, though sadly drawn into permanent melancholy, began to sparkle with renewed hope. Finally he clapped his hands in silent rejoicing and rubbed the area over his heart as if his spirits were lifting. Then he pulled from inside his torn coat a large red cardboard heart—whole and unblemished. Shyly he offered his tribute; tearfully Savvy accepted it.

"You want us to be together . . . forever?" When he nodded, she smiled absurdly. She had been waiting a lifetime for that declaration. "Oh, darling, it's what I want too."

Sky gently kissed her fingertips and pledged his undying love by pulsating his hands over his heart, showing Savvy that it beat only for her. Overjoyed, she unfastened the tethers of his balloon companions, giggling with silly comments and real emotion as she let one and then another float free to the ceiling.

She tapped the police whistle. "I'll bet you had some hangover, huh?" His look of misery as he rolled his eyes heavenward and cradled his head brought gentle laughter to her lips.

She looked at him through the magnifying glass and caught a broad, sexy wink. "I *do* love you, you know that, don't you?" He grinned from ear to ear at her proclamation.

Twiddling with the semaphore flags, she hastened to add, "And I need you too." He jabbed his chest with his thumb and held up two fingers, miming "Me too!"

Releasing all but the last string, she toyed with the

sad little clown doll and whispered throatily, "This week hasn't been any fun at all, Skylar Brady."

Unable to resist any longer, Sky pulled her into his arms and kissed her with everything he had in him. "Can we please kiss and make up now?" he asked.

She laughed in total relief. "It's a little late to ask, isn't it?"

"Oh, baby," he crooned, feeling the hurt of their days of separation fade. "I haven't even known which end was up this week. I'm so sorry I caused you all this pain. But I was so damn scared that it wouldn't work out. Not because you didn't love me or because I didn't love you," he hastened to explain. "I just didn't think I'd get to keep you for the rest of my life."

Tenderly Savvy removed his battered hat and torn gloves, pushing off his coat and dropping it in a heap on the floor. "You're stuck with me now, Brady. We're a team for ever and a day . . . *and I mean it!*" she emphasized, pushing him toward the bathroom door.

"I'm in complete agreement with that, partner."

They showered together, lavishly shampooing one another's hair and smoothing thick layers of lather all over their bodies. By the time they were rinsed clean, both were breathing so raggedly that neither wanted to take the time to towel the moisture from their bodies. Suddenly it seemed imperative that they make sweet and glorious love to seal their lifelong commitment . . . this time permanently.

Savvy nestled in his warm embrace when he lifted her into his arms and carried her to her bed. Together they fell across the mattress, unwilling, perhaps unable, to release their hold. With gentle fire

Sky lapped the remaining droplets from her skin, making blazing paths from her throat to the tips of her toes. She writhed beneath his hot, aroused body, feeling his soft body hair tickle and excite her flesh. Then as his touch grew more bold, urging her to come with him to their vital time of release, she prepared the way, opening her body to the molten passion that he offered.

"Now, Sky, darling," she cried, lifting her hips to meet his thrust. "Make me forget our separation."

He moved faster. Harder and harder he ground into her, murmuring words that to Savvy sounded like pure erotica. "Come fly with me, my love. Come up into the sky and experience the universe."

"Yes, oh, yes," she cried, feeling herself pulled deeper into his convulsive embrace. "You are my world . . . my universe . . . *you are my Sky!*"

Their accelerating shouts of rejoicing echoed inside the darkened room. The two voices intermingled as their bodies entwined in the final moment. Sighing and murmuring words of love, both rode the light side of love to the edge of tomorrow, where they lay, bathed in the mist of their journey and their tears. No man or woman ever felt so happy and at peace.

Later, while they renewed their plans for the future, and in particular reinstated the canceled dinner party, Sky grinned over at his Savvy and laughed out loud. His happiness knew no bounds. He was with the woman he loved even beyond his own life. "Hey, pretty lady," he exclaimed, nestling his blond head against the valley between her breasts. "How long were you going to keep the bombardment going?" He snickered against her skin, making her squirm in delight.

"I swore I was going to give you the full treatment . . . seven days."

"I only got six," he said, enjoying the feel of her body wiggling beneath his as he sucked deeply on one of her rosy smoke-tinted nipples. "What was the last one?"

Laughing breathlessly, she gently pushed him aside and rolled to her feet to pick up the remaining box. She handed it to him, and her snapping eyes warned him that he should get ready.

He unwrapped the box carefully, complimenting Savvy on her expert packaging and secretly enjoying her growing agitation as he took his own sweet time with it. When the balloon burst forth, Sky caught it by its tail and stared at the pair of baby booties dangling right before his wide, surprised eyes. The message almost drove him right through the ceiling! "Have you checked your calendar lately?" it read.

He flew to his feet and grabbed Savvy, forcing her to look him straight in the eyes. "*Are* you pregnant, honey?" She savored his torment. He was half delirious with joy and half worried to death because he'd caused her such suffering during these last several days. "Savvy," he whispered hoarsely, "*are we pregnant*?"

She couldn't torture him another second and broke into a cheerful smile. "Nope!"

Instantly Sky collapsed onto the bed with Savvy in his arms. "I don't know if I'm sad that we're not or mad because we aren't," he lamented, still pulling in large draughts of oxygen. "Why the hell would you do a thing like that, Savena Alexander, almost Brady?"

She cuddled against him, reveling in the clean smell of his skin, nearly faint from the feel of him beneath her. "I figured that message would either bring you to me . . . or send you running for the hills," she explained, moaning softly when he began to explore some of her erogenous zones. "It was a crazy idea, Sky. I'd never try to trap you, darling."

Sky continued to excite and massage her responsive body until she could no longer lie still and began to push against his throbbing masculinity. As if she were weightless, Sky lifted her over his aroused flesh and settled her across his gyrating hips. He pulled her down to kiss her with his usual mastery while her body began to move without her consent. Then he whispered hotly against her ear, sending flames of desire coursing through her limbs.

"It's not such a crazy idea," he said thoughtfully. "Honey, I surrender." He fitted her body around his and began to lift and pull her to him with passionate, thrusting movements. His eyes, which she noted with fascination had changed suddenly to smoldering indigo blue, locked with hers in a challenging, burning gaze. "Come on, Savvy," he dared. *"Trap me!"*

EDITOR'S CORNER

Did you ever harbor a secret desire to be able to pick a lock with a hairpin? crack a safe? outwit a cunning mastermind? I sure have—especially when my front door key sticks in the lock . . . when I can't even wrench open the cabinet in the tool shed . . . uh, and about that cunning mastermind, I have to confess we've been having a bit of trouble at home convincing our puppy that she isn't boss of the house!

Well, if you too have fantasized about having some of the skills of a female 007, you are going to be mad about Kay Hooper's Troy Bennett in **ILLEGAL POSSESSION**, LOVESWEPT #83. You know Kay's wonderful romances so, even if you aren't a fan of derring-do traits in your heroines, I predict that still you'll love this entrancing book. Troy relishes the thrills in her unusual line of work while avoiding anything even remotely dangerous in matters of the heart. Then she encounters the sexy, powerful, and upstanding, almost self-righteous Dallas Cameron. Blinking red lights . . . emotional danger for Troy and trouble for the scrupulous Dallas. But they can't resist one another! Just how these two delightfully different people mellow and change to accommodate each other provides a love story you won't soon forget!

BJ James's romance next month, **A STRANGER CALLED ADAM**, LOVESWEPT #84, is breathtakingly dramatic from first until last. An aura of mystery pervades Shadow Mountain and touches all who live beneath it. And no one is more touched by that mystery than Tracy Walker. One of the few who dares to challenge the mountain, who even lives on it, Tracy has a fascinating past and a challenging future . . .

(continued)

especially after she has rescued the daughter of Adam Grayson. Adam instantly recognizes Tracy from long ago and almost as quickly is captivated by her. But Shadow Mountain, like a living, breathing creature, looms between them—representing all that separates these two loving people from happiness together. BJ's love story, shimmering with passionate intensity, is indeed a memorable read.

I must say that the day Joan Elliott Pickart's first manuscript (unsolicited and I believe, addressed simply "Dear Editor") arrived in this office was a lucky day for all of us who love romance of humor, passion, and touching emotion. Nowhere will you find those qualities more evident tha in Joan's **ALL THE TO-MORROWS,** LOVESWEPT #85. The first meeting between Dr. Sheridan Todd and Mr. David Cavelli is unusual, to put it mildly. The story swerves from the zany to a deeply touching account of the growing love and passion between Sheridan and David, especially as he tries to help her adopt the deaf child she cherishes and longs to mother. His intervention on her behalf in legal proceedings boomerangs and temporary custody of four-year-old Dominic is awarded to David. This most sensitive, loving man has only one flaw: a phobia about marriage. You'll be holding your breath between chuckles as you experience the delightful resolution of **ALL THE TOMORROWS**.

Now, rounding out this wonderful quartet of romance novels is Iris Johansen's **BLUE VELVET,** LOVESWEPT #86. If you guessed that Iris was going to give you Beau Lantry's love story, you were right on target! We rediscover Beau in a somewhat sleazy bar in a port town on a Caribbean Island. (Don't worry! Beau still only sips ginger ale!) His yacht is moored at the dock and he's out on the town for the evening. But any plans he might have been forming for the night come to a screeching end when Kate Gilbert enters the bar. Courage and heart are qualities Kate has in abundance; being sensible and calculating the consequences of acts are qualities she has in rather short supply! Beau to the rescue as a modern day knight on a white yacht, though Kate hardly sees herself as a damsel in distress. More often it's poor Beau who finds himself in distress as she embroils them in one hair-raising episode after another. For example, just imagine how drug runners respond when Kate destroys their cache of more than a million dollars' worth of cocaine . . . not to mention the reaction of corrupt cops when she sends two of their number off for a short nap with wine lightly laced with sleeping tablets. And through it all— even during high-speed chases at sea—the incredibly innocent and ridiculously brave Kate is capturing Beau's heart . . . just as she will yours. **BLUE VELVET** is one of Iris's most charming and madcap romps. Enjoy!

As always, thanks for your warm letters. We love hearing from you. With every good wish,
Sincerely,

Carolyn Nichols

Carolyn Nichols
  Editor
LOVESWEPT
Bantam Books, Inc.
666 Fifth Avenue
New York, NY 10103

P.S. In case you missed the on sale date last month of Sandra Brown's marvelous historical, **SUNSET EMBRACE,** do remember to ask your bookseller for it when you go in to get this month's LOVESWEPTS!

A special excerpt of
the remarkable new novel
by the author of
A Many-Splendoured Thing and **Till Morning Comes**

The Enchantress

by Han Suyin

Dear Reader:

I'm delighted to announce the upcoming publication of Han Suyin's most recent novel, THE ENCHANTRESS, an unforgettable tale of rich romance and intrigue set in Switzerland, China, and Thailand in the eighteenth century. It's a remarkable book, a sumptuous feast of the sights and sounds of a time gone by. And it's a story that only Han Suyin, whose life has spanned East and West, could tell.

Enter a hidden world. Travel with Han Suyin to the eighteenth century, a time when the distinctions between magic, science, and the mystical spirits were far less clear than in our modern age. Meet adventurous Colin and his lovely twin sister Bea, whose Celtic ancestry has given them the Gift—the ability to hear each other's unspoken thoughts, especially in times of danger.

Sail with them to distant China, where Colin is called upon to repair the Emperor's magnificent clocks. On the way, see the city of Marseilles, sparkling between sun and water. Feel the caress of the wind at dawn. Breathe the perfumed scent of sandalwood and jasmine. And then, at journey's end, look in wonder at the glistening golden spires of Ayuthia as Colin and Bea enter the radiant city. Here, in splendor beyond their imagining, brother and sister will find greater love than each has ever known—and endure greater loss before Fate reveals what awaits them.

A bestselling author who's as charming as the stories she so skillfully tells, Han Suyin researches her books in China, the land of her birth, Switzerland, and India. THE ENCHANTRESS is sure to delight her millions of already devoted readers as well as win the hearts of new ones.

With the whisper of a delicate brush on silk paper, Han Suyin brings you into Ayuthia, the Enchantress, a world you will never forget.

With warm regards,

Tessa Rapoport
Senior Editor

Colin and Bea still tell the story of THE ENCHANTRESS in alternating voices, Bea's in italics. In this excerpt, they have reached Ayuthia. Colin (called Keran here) is about to wrestle with Chiprasong for the love of Jit, a woman whose name Colin does not yet know but who has won his heart. Prince Udorn, Colin's loyal friend, is the man Bea will marry, although she does not love him. Join them now as they begin their new life.

THE MATCHES WERE TO be held on the small plain of Bang Paket across the river, not far from the French settlement and its square-towered stone church of Saint Joseph. A large, happy crowd milled round the flat tamped field. The boxers and Krabi-Krabong swordsmen were ready. Chiprasong was already there, in a plain *pannung* or loincloth, his skin glistening with sandalwood oil. I think he wanted to be popular, to be known to the people as a simple man, perhaps to emulate the regretted King Boromakot, who often went among his people, clad as a commoner. Udorn and I sat down among the crowd, and the boxing began.

It was then, looking up, that I saw her, on the terrace of one of the stilt houses that lined one side of the field. She was with two older women, their hair shorn, and in black. She had turned her head to speak to one of them, and then she was looking at the crowd, as if looking for someone, and she saw me. I stared until I remembered that this meant scorn, and lowered my head, bringing it back to the boxers. Chiprasong had lifted his leg high to knock his opponent to the ground, but the latter, a limber young man and a fraction swifter, took a flying leap to bring Chiprasong to the ground. But Chiprasong stepped sideways and the young man missed.

I looked again, quickly glancing up. She was no longer on the terrace, and my heart began to pound wildly, as if I had lost an immense treasure. Oh let me see her but once again, oh let me see her . . . and then I did see her, she was on the outer edge of the circling crowd just opposite me and she was looking at me.

I did not know that I was in love then; only that the earth had changed under me, that my mind was wiped clean of everything else. Her face, her shoulders, the smallness and perfection of her. In a land where so many women were loveliness incarnate, it seemed to me that no one else but she alone was beautiful, truly so. Was she noble, was she a commoner? She wore the day's color, green for Wednesday, the *jongkra-bane* and top-tied halter as women at work did to keep their hands and legs free.

How could I approach her?

Udorn was bending over me. "Keran, Keran, are you dreaming? Chiprasong would like to have a round with you."

The sun was westering, its pink glow filled the sky, rose of a pearl. It touched her hair, her mouth. She wore a pink hibiscus in her hair.

Chiprasong strode up to me, assumed a boxing

stance, calling out something that made the crowd laugh. I felt hot all over.

"You cannot refuse; this is a friendly match. Better let him win quickly, so you will not be hurt." Udorn's voice was a little anxious. He replied gaily, however, and I knew that he was trying to make the crowd laugh at something else.

But the crowd really wanted some clowning now, to finish the day. Perhaps to see Chiprasong knock down a *farang*. There would be no dishonor in losing to the Tiger man, Prince Chiprasong.

No dishonor. Except that she was there. I could not be made a mockery of. I could not let Chiprasong beat me. She would see that I was lame when I stood up to fight. . . .

"The *farang* way, of course," he shouted.

As before any match, there was a short invocation, a gathering of the forces of the spirit and body, and then Chiprasong danced towards me, light on his feet, his knotted fists beautiful, almost caressing the air. He meant, I knew, to knock me down a few times, in as ridiculous a posture as possible, to draw laughter. He was grinning in a friendly manner. I hated him.

Watch his feet. He always feints with his right fist, kicks by wheeling his left foot. His big toe is lethal.

He came, lunging a deft right, a quick left, but I had already turned, letting his punch slide on my raised shoulder, and with my club foot hooked his ankle, while he was carried forwards by the momentum of his blow, and I whirled away from the impact of his body.

He stumbled but caught himself, and from a half-bent position swung once again towards my belly; but I had turned round on myself, and I was now behind him while he went forwards and fell on his back as I slammed his left arm backwards. . . .

He reeled and I seized his drooping wrist, twisting it hard and twisting him with it. Then with my good leg as a solid pillar I used my club foot to kick the back of the other knee. He fell then, and as he fell I chopped him in the neck with my free hand, a murderous blow.

He would not be up again for a while. I had tried to kill him. I had forgotten what Traveler had said: "Only self-defense, not to kill . . ."

She had seen that I was lame.

Udorn was handing me my tunic and my shoes, wiping the sweat off me. He was beaming, for I had won. "I did not know that you possessed the mastery of Zen," he said. "You keep secret many a thing, Keran."

I put on my cloth shoes, the one with a solid inner sole higher than the other first.

Men and women were pressing around me with joined hands, girls garlanding me with flowers. And she was there, smiling up at me; softly, shyly, her hands placed a garland round my neck.

The drums began. Double-headed *Tapone*, *Song-Na*, *Klong-Thad*, all the tunes of the Thai people, with their recall of hooves in the forest, of echoing tiger roar. Calling to the feast. The people of three villages had gathered, they squatted on palm leaves or on the ground. Men in black went about with pitchers of palm wine, carried vats of steaming food.

. . . Such a feast. Men coming to salute me, to ask me where I had learnt my fighting.

"Truly, tonight you are the *wang*, king of the feast," Udorn said exultingly.

Two women fanned me zealously throughout my eating, and on rattan trays in front of me were laid many bowls. I drank and ate, drank the hot palm wine. And then the dancing began.

The musicians arranged themselves in a circle, and

the drums now went sweet, precise and soft, like the pulse of night, like the beat of blood, a night so soft it was almost painful to be alive, to know that such nights are not given forever. The men rose to dance, and also the women, and she was there too, in the ranks of the women, until the thickening press of dancers hid her from my sight.

Drums. The night throbbed with them, and with the sound of the *pinai* flutes rising like nightingales, throaty and shrill and calling to the forest to listen.

Dancing—long weaving files of men, and across from them on the other side of the field, the women almost immobile save for the slow, ritual movement of the arms, the hands, the necks; meditative, weaving the spell of the enchanted night. Offering praise to the Lords of the Spirit for the goodness of the evening, the feast, the dance. . . .

And because of the palm wine emboldening me I made my way through the ranks of women until I found her, and folded my hands and bowed my head in front of her. We danced, five feet away from each other. She did not look at me, nor I at her; I kept my eyes down. Only my hands, my arms, said: I love you, I love you. The world has suddenly become a rainbow, become fragrant, delectable, because of you. Oh let me but love you, my hands said, weaving the air.

"Her name is Jit," Udorn told me when we were back in our *polun*, the rowers calling out the strokes. We were through the *Nei Kai*, the Chinese gate, which could always be opened, even at night.

"I shall die, Udorn, if I can't have her," I said. "Not my body, but something within me will die."

"Ah, the thunder and lightning of love is worse than any typhoon," Udorn said. "She is the daughter of a small official; she has Chinese blood in her, as well as Thai."

"I love her. That is all."

"Let me arrange it. You are not secretive, Keran. Everyone could see you were in love. Even Chiprasong saw it. He recovered from his faint and he was watching. I think he is angry because you shamed him. But now he should understand that it was because of love. You could not lose in front of her."

The rowers' oar blades whisked the water, pulling smoothly, beating time. Time, in slow oar beats, in slow heartbeats. Time had brought me here. I heard the croaking of the night frogs delighting in the watery night.

"Udorn, if she but come to me, I shall be the most blessed of men."

*   *   *

Anno Domini 1763–1764

I married Udorn at an auspicious hour in January of 1763. The ceremonies lasted three days. I changed my clothes twenty-one times, each time with a new set of jewels. Abdul Reza's generosity was unstinted; Udorn covered me with gifts. I now had five large chests of China lacquer with hinges and locks of pure gold, filled with jewelry and gold-threaded garments. And salvers and vases and boxes of gold, silver, enamel, ivory, and mother-of-pearl, enough to fill seven large cupboards.

Udorn is handsome. He has proved himself skilled and courteous as a lover. Since I do not love him I can all the more appreciate the pleasure he gives me. I keep intact the weather of my soul, and move towards my own freedom, undeterred, sovereign.

I think of the strong and bitter woman sitting in the Forbidden City of Peking: the Mother, Empress Dowager, who killed her son's love because she would not let him betray the Empire.

Perhaps she sometimes thinks of me.

Colin. Between my brother and me is a bond we must both maintain and resist. We have to shut our minds away from each other, since now we both have lovers; and we shall have to live with this interdiction all our lives. Perhaps others do, who bury deep within themselves their lust and hunger for a sister, a mother, to be more than sister or mother. With my brother and me it is a shallow grave, in which part of ourselves must lie forever.

Colin's love is a maiden shy and gentle, whose uncompli- cated mind, like a rose, emits a wordless happiness. Whose body is slight, pliant, beautiful. She sees a bird and thinks: This is a bird. She goes no further, but to her the bird is all delight, marvel, joy. She will never grow weary of everyday small miracles. She has neither ambition nor malice. She wants only to serve Colin, to love him. This is her destiny.

Colin and I now speak words to each other, engage in philosophical discussions. He argues that time is a function of the universe; and that Newton has proved that time goes on, even if no one is there to make clocks, to measure time. I say that time shrinks or stretches according to the grip of our souls and the desire of our bodies. "Then you don't believe in my watches." Colin grins, looking young and boyish because he is happy.

In Newton's world are no spirits of tree and fire and enchanted forest. But here in Ayuthia are spirits everywhere, potent and powerful.

"Colin, the android you are thinking of making, he must be a king. He must have a king's face."

"The King?"

"Not Ekatat. Someone else. As yet I do not see his face. When I do, I shall make the face for you."

On the tenth day after our wedding I tell Udorn to bring

back his other wives. "They will grieve without you. Your heart is mine, so I am not jealous."

Udorn is delighted. A nobleman with only one wife is a pitiful thing in Ayuthia. Three of them are back; their speech the twitter of sparrows, their manners charming. "Three is enough," I say, and Udorn laughs, and calls me an enchantress, the queen of his heart.

The Gift is strong within me here, for Ayuthia is both dream and reality, fusion of everything contradictory, diverse, wayward, mutable.

"There will be war again, Udorn. The Burmese will come again."

"I know it, most beloved." He sighs. He and his cousin Phya Cham are anxious and so is the Kalahom, for the ramparts of Ayuthia are in a poor state. Its many forts need repairs. There are no cannon balls for the cannon installed by the Portuguese under King Boromakot, Ekatat's father, some twenty years ago. Ekatat refuses to release the cannon and ammunition stored in the royal armory to strengthen the defense forts. The muskets of the palace guards have not been fired in many years.

King Ekatat is besotted with shamans and exorcists who feed him philters, love potions, and quicksilver to make him invisible and invincible, so that, it is said, his teeth are beginning to drop away.

Udorn sighs. And nothing is done.

I go to see Abdul Reza in his house in the Muslim quarter with my retinue of maids and women fighters, Amazons trained to protect other women. I order them to withdraw. "I have important matters to talk over with Prince Reza." Now they know that I can do all I want—I am not fettered as other women are—and they leave me alone.

Abdul Reza sits, dignified, tormented. A man. A man with the smell and savor of a man. He reminds me of the

Chinese Emperor Tsienlung. He is the same age, with a body seasoned and inured with living and many women. I feel the stir of lust in me.

"I am yours, Lord Reza, if you so wish. For now I am no longer your ward, and I can choose the men I wish to make love with." His lips go pale. He moistens them.

"Lady, I cannot cheat."

"Udorn does not own me. I own myself."

His hands grip the small knife he wears always at his belt.

"You are wicked, immoral," he says, in a measured voice. "You play with people . . . you are cruel, Lady Bea."

"Wicked, cruel, immoral? Because I please myself, as a man pleases himself with women?"

A week later, he becomes mine, and pleasures me greatly, for he has a wonderful body, spare, undiminished by age; passion and anger make him fierce, indefatigable.

"You have taken my manhood from me," he says afterwards.

"But we shall always remember this hour," I reply. "For we were truthful with each other, were we not?"

A Dazzling New Novel

Scents

by
Johanna Kingsley

They were the fabulous Jolays, half sisters, bound by blood but not by love. Daughters of an outstanding French perfumer whose world had collapsed, now they are bitter rivals, torn apart by their personal quests for power. It was the luminous Vie who created an empire, but it was the sensuous, rebellious Marty who was determined to control it. No matter what the cost, she would conquer Vie's glittering world and claim it as her own . . .

Buy SCENTS, on sale December 15, 1984, wherever Bantam paperbacks are sold, or use the handy coupon below for ordering:

AN EXQUISITELY ROMANTIC NOVEL UNLIKE
ANY OTHER LOVE STORY YOU HAVE EVER READ

Chase the Moon

by
Catherine Nicholson

For Corrie Modena, only one man shares her dreams, a
stranger whom she has never met face to face and whom she
knows only as "Harlequin." Over the years, his letters sus-
tain her—encouraging, revealing, increasingly intimate. And
when Corrie journeys to Paris to pursue her music, she
knows that she will also be searching for her beloved
Harlequin. . . .

Buy CHASE THE MOON, on sale November 15, 1984,
wherever Bantam paperbacks are sold, or use the handy
coupon below for ordering:

LOVESWEPT

Love Stories you'll never forget by authors you'll always remember

☐	21603	**Heaven's Price #1** Sandra Brown	$1.95
☐	21604	**Surrender #2** Helen Mittermeyer	$1.95
☐	21600	**The Joining Stone #3** Noelle Berry McCue	$1.95
☐	21601	**Silver Miracles #4** Fayrene Preston	$1.95
☐	21605	**Matching Wits #5** Carla Neggers	$1.95
☐	21606	**A Love for All Time #6** Dorothy Garlock	$1.95
☐	21609	**Hard Drivin' Man #10** Nancy Carlson	$1.95
☐	21610	**Beloved Intruder #11** Noelle Berry McCue	$1.95
☐	21611	**Hunter's Payne #12** Joan J. Domning	$1.95
☐	21618	**Tiger Lady #13** Joan Domning	$1.95
☐	21613	**Stormy Vows #14** Iris Johansen	$1.95
☐	21614	**Brief Delight #15** Helen Mittermeyer	$1.95
☐	21616	**A Very Reluctant Knight #16** Billie Green	$1.95
☐	21617	**Tempest at Sea #17** Iris Johansen	$1.95
☐	21619	**Autumn Flames #18** Sara Orwig	$1.95
☐	21620	**Pfarr Lake Affair #19** Joan Domning	$1.95
☐	21621	**Heart on a String #20** Carla Neggars	$1.95
☐	21622	**The Seduction of Jason #21** Fayrene Preston	$1.95
☐	21623	**Breakfast In Bed #22** Sandra Brown	$1.95
☐	21624	**Taking Savannah #23** Becky Combs	$1.95
☐	21625	**The Reluctant Lark #24** Iris Johansen	$1.95

Prices and availability subject to change without notice.

Buy them at your local bookstore or use this handy coupon for ordering:

Bantam Books, Inc., Dept. SW, 414 East Golf Road, Des Plaines, Ill. 60016

Please send me the books I have checked above. I am enclosing $_____ (please add $1.25 to cover postage and handling). Send check or money order—no cash or C.O.D.'s please.

Mr/Ms_____

Address _____

City/State_____ Zip_____

SW—12/84

Please allow four to six weeks for delivery. This offer expires 6/85.

LOVESWEPT

Love Stories you'll never forget by authors you'll always remember

☐	21630	Lightning That Lingers #25 Sharon & Tom Curtis	$1.95
☐	21631	Once In a Blue Moon #26 Billie J. Green	$1.95
☐	21632	The Bronzed Hawk #27 Iris Johansen	$1.95
☐	21637	Love, Catch a Wild Bird #28 Anne Reisser	$1.95
☐	21626	The Lady and the Unicorn #29 Iris Johansen	$1.95
☐	21628	Winner Take All #30 Nancy Holder	$1.95
☐	21635	The Golden Valkyrie #31 Iris Johansen	$1.95
☐	21638	C.J.'s Fate #32 Kay Hooper	$1.95
☐	21639	The Planting Season #33 Dorothy Garlock	$1.95
☐	21629	For Love of Sami #34 Fayrene Preston	$1.95
☐	21627	The Trustworthy Redhead #35 Iris Johansen	$1.95
☐	21636	A Touch of Magic #36 Carla Neggers	$1.95
☐	21641	Irresistible Forces #37 Marie Michael	$1.95
☐	21642	Temporary Angel #38 Billie Green	$1.95
☐	21646	Kirsten's Inheritance #39 Joan Domning	$2.25
☐	21645	Return to Santa Flores #40 Iris Johansen	$2.25
☐	21656	The Sophisticated Mountain Gal #41 Joan Bramsch	$2.25
☐	21655	Heat Wave #42 Sara Orwig	$2.25
☐	21649	To See the Daisies . . . First #43 Billie Green	$2.25
☐	21648	No Red Roses #44 Iris Johansen	$2.25
☐	21644	That Old Feeling #45 Fayrene Preston	$2.25
☐	21650	Something Different #46 Kay Hooper	$2.25

Prices and availability subject to change without notice.